HAUNTING
MISS FENWICK

ALINA K. FIELD

Dedication

To the dedicated women of the
School Sisters of Notre Dame,
who committed their lives to wrangling and
teaching children like me, and especially to Sister
Mary Cyprian who taught me the art of
diagramming a sentence!

*While he's haunting Miss Fenwick,
Miss Fenwick haunts him.*

Thrilled to finally have a permanent home, a Squire's daughter won't let a supernatural creature scare her away. While hunting the ghost she doesn't believe in, she stumbles upon a mysterious flesh and blood man who might be the key to all of her problems.

When the new Squire moves into Fenwick Manor, an ex-army officer secretly searching the sprawling medieval wreck devises a plan. First, the manor's legendary ghost will chase servants away. Then, he'll convince the new residents to leave.

But the Squire's spirited daughter soon has him wondering if he might have found a perfect comrade in arms to help battle old enemies and find the proof that will clear his family name.

CHAPTER ONE

Yorkshire, 1822

The fresh folk were underfoot again.

Captain Frederick George Sanderford—Freddy to friends and family—vanished into the overgrown hedgerow.

Hell and damnation, he'd spent the last two days dodging the new residents of Fenwick Manor. The new squire's surprise arrival had disrupted his plans just as he'd got a sense of the lay of the land.

And now, the woman was eying the door of the narrow shed propped at the back of the hill, atop which the manor house had perched for centuries. She commenced jiggling the latch, pushing, and yanking it.

A tall lass, she was, and no tender miss, yet the lock didn't budge. It was sturdy. He'd just barely had time to make sure of it.

She paused, looked around, and paced back and forth through the ankle high brush fronting the wee structure. A ring of keys emerged from her pocket. One-by-one, she poked each stick of metal into the lock. They didn't work, as he knew they wouldn't. That was one key she would be missing.

Her hands went to a tidy waist, accentuating shapely hips.

"*Blast it.*" A stout boot shot out, shaking the structure.

A laugh gurgled out of him, and she spun around. Dark hair sprang out from under her bonnet, and her eyes flashed a blue so true he could see it at twenty paces.

Hell. He caught his breath. He'd not had a proper glimpse of the squire's daughter before. Her name was Tilly. That much he knew from hearing the old man bellowing for her and her calling back "*What, Papa?*".

Tilly was lovely.

Caught out anyway, he stepped out of the brush, tugging off his hat and fumbling it with proper servility, like one of his family's servants or a soldier serving under him. Footman or footslog, 'twas as good a disguise as any for a man seeking to avoid notice. And never mind the temptations she offered, catching too much of her notice might risk his plans.

"Beg pardon, miss," he said.

She blinked, and her gaze darted around.

Ach, lass, you've just realized there's no one to come should you need rescuing. The squire would be ensconced in his library, the new servants—well, if they were still there, they'd not hear her scream.

Above them, Fenwick Manor was all but deserted, and across the narrow path the meadow stretched, its stone fences crumbling up against unkempt hedges that fronted the dense woods. The late Sir Richard Fenwick should have been shot for more than his murderous ways—it was a crime the way he'd neglected his land and his holdings. This woman was strong, but she'd be no match for the work.

She'd be no match for him, either, but he wasn't a danger to her. He was, after all, a gentleman.

He stood quietly, waiting. The army had taught him that, sure enough. Even an officer had to grovel sometimes.

"Who are you?" she asked, forthrightly, "and what are you doing on Sir Newton's land?"

Ah. *Sir Newton* was her papa's name. A distant cousin to the late Sir Richard, Sir Newton was the lucky heir to the Fenwick estate, such a valuable piece of Yorkshire coast, so close to the smuggling runs, so spotted with caverns and hideaways.

"Passin' through is all, miss." He spread his hands wide. "Not poachin', I swear."

She blinked again, and that hard gaze softened. "Are you hungry?"

His chest tightened and something inside him stirred. He'd seen damnable hunger in the last many years, both during the wars and in the time since: men unable to work, unable to buy food for their families, and the penalty for poaching a mere rabbit or hare might be death.

The lass had a heart to match her bonny looks.

"Because, you see, I'm hiring men. Women as well, to work at the manor. Grooms, laborers, maids. Have you a wife, or…or a sister, or a daughter in Clampton?"

Clampton was the nearby village he'd been avoiding. "No, none of those. And I'm not needing to addle some brass."

"Excuse me?"

"Earn wages. I'm not in need of work, miss. Good day to you."

He turned, plunged through the hedgerow and moved into the trees, stopping to catch his breath.

Miss Tilly was not what he'd expected.

And what had he expected? Years earlier, he'd had his turn with a lady, a jilt who'd decided waiting for a man in the King's service was too much to ask. But he'd wager Miss Tilly was made of sterner stuff, or his name wasn't Freddy Sanderford.

Sterner stuff, and curves that would fill a man's hand nicely.

The thought stirred other parts of him, and he shook it off. He'd been too long without a woman, was all and...

Laughter burst from him. The squire's daughter wanted to hire *him*, poor lass. The only work he'd be about was finding the proof needed to bring his brother back and bloody the culprits involved in his false arrest. It was a pity Sir Richard was already dead.

He doubled back, and when he reached the path, spotted the lass's bonnet bobbing along up the hill to the Manor. As soon as she'd disappeared from view, he fitted his key to the lock in the door and slipped in.

CHAPTER TWO

Two days later

A crash filled the stable yard below and a buxom woman raced from the kitchens, her apron flapping along with her arms.

"He's 'ere," she shrieked.

The woodchopper dropped his axe while two more women rushed out of the manor, one grabbing for the arm of the stable boy who'd come out of the barn to gawk.

From his perch in an attic dormer, Freddy couldn't help but chuckle. Devious, it was, but effective in clearing intruders.

In short order the sniveling gudgeons moved their huddle away from the haunted manor. They'd reached the gate when a new figure rushed out.

Freddy pressed his nose to the wavy glass. It was the lass, Tilly. Her work apron twisted over dun-colored skirts, and her uncovered locks flew about escaping their pins.

"*Come back*," she shouted.

The battle cry could be heard in the next county. The old Squire should have named her Boudica. Fierce Boudica rallying her reluctant rabble. She was bloody magnificent.

Hopping muddy ruts, she rushed the motley villagers who squared up like infantry defending against a cavalry assault.

Their tactic worked. Tilly halted, propping her hands on her hips.

"It was only the dog knocking things about. Come back to work." The marshal tones bounced off the stone walls of the stables.

The stout maid, first bearer of news, pushed through the line and plopped *her* hands on her much more expansive hips. "No, miss, it *weren't* and we *won't*."

Even from here, he could see Tilly's back stiffen. Height versus width—if it came down to blows, it might be a close match.

Another woman's finger shot out, and he spotted the dog trotting up to join Tilly. "'Tis the hound of hell, anyway, that beast is." The words shrieked up the crumbling bricks and along the rotting timbers.

"Don't be ridiculous," Tilly said.

"Don't matter 'bout the dog." That was the woodchopper. "Sir Richard be real, and we best be leaving."

"Sir Richard is *dead*," Boudica cried. "Gone these many months. Buried in London. Not coming back." She took a step after them. "Please, good people," she wheedled, "my father has said a powerful blessing over this house. I assure you, *there are no ghosts here*."

The villagers vanished from view, and as the seconds ticked by, her proud shoulders sagged.

A dribble of shame slithered through him. If it weren't for his need to right a terrible wrong, if it weren't for that, Sir Richard would go back to his place in Hades and leave her in peace.

But justice demanded he find the means to finish this personal mission. Serving King and country had taken his best years, and he was finished with that. Serving his family—his brother, his mother—came first now.

Cowed down by the servants' desertions, she stumbled and turned back to the house, fair on to crying. *Gad*, he couldn't abide the sight of a woman's tears.

A drop of rain slapped the pane, and he turned away.

For certain, she and her scribbling father would have to leave before All Hallows. Managing the remote Fenwick Manor through a Yorkshire winter would be too much for the two of them, a superstitious old dreamer and a young woman—strapping and fine though she might be.

He rubbed his hands together. With this new batch of servants gone, he could move a bit quicker with his search of the manor.

A roar filled the courtyard and rattled the windows and then came a shriek.

What the devil. Was she in danger?

He rushed back to the window in time to see wood split and fly.

Good God. The lass hadn't succumbed to despair. The only tears were the drops pouring down from the heavens. Boudica had picked up the axe and was unleashing her fury on stout logs.

He'd best stay even deeper out of her way.

*****

"*Blast.*"

Matilda Fenwick crashed the axe down, splitting the wood cleanly. Out of one piece, a whorled knot projected like a pig's snout, putting her in mind of the shabby canvas she'd found in a storeroom, a portrait of Fenwick Manor's last baronet, Sir Richard.

She arranged the body on the chopping block.

Sir Bloody Richard Fenwick was not coming back to Fenwick Manor.

"*No—*" She raised the axe. "*Blasted—*" The axe hung in the air for a few vibrating seconds. "*Ghosts.*"

Whoosh and *Crash*. The blade split the torso, this time not cleanly. A piece like an arm flew off, and a flurry erupted. With an excited *woof* Wulver retrieved the limb and plopped down on her haunches, the piece of wood lodged firmly between her teeth.

Tilly leaned on the axe, reaching for calm, and fondled the dog's black woolly head with its streak of white. "Oh, Wulver, you're filled with burrs." One didn't keep the giant dog contained for long. The lovely girl had been out exploring the nearby woods again.

"You are not a devil dog." Bending close, she whispered, "Your namesake is known to be kindly." And, to be safe, she'd sneaked the woolly black pup into the sanctuary of Papa's last church for a proper baptism. She would swear it had helped with the spirited girl's training.

Perhaps there was more along that line that she could do here. Like Papa, she had faith, but unlike him, she had no superstitions. Well, few, anyway. Her faith was the pragmatic sort. If a rite might calm a wild puppy or a grown person, there was no sense in not trying it. Tucked among the dusty works of Cicero in the library at Fenwick Manor, she'd found a book of papist prayers, all in Latin. The Rite of Exorcism had been included.

The villagers might find it worthwhile.

Wulver shuffled on her forepaws, her wiggling tail threatening to catapult her out of her sit, happiness gurgling and foaming around the piece of wood.

Tilly took the dog's offering and tossed it to the pile of cut wood, sighing. "It's not enough." Papa might not mind the cold while he worked into the night in the cavernous library, but the days were growing chillier while he grew thinner. He would need more fuel than this.

While Wulver ran off to nose about in the brush, she gathered the chopped wood and shifted it onto the sheltered pile, and then picked up the axe again.

Her muscles would ache tomorrow, but it wasn't as though she'd never cut wood, never tended their two horses, never toted buckets and trays and laundry. She'd worked at the vicarage alongside first her mother and then their maid-of-all-work, and since their arrival in Yorkshire, she'd done nothing but physical labor, thanks to the ghost of Sir Richard and his ill-kept manor.

The main building dated to the sixteenth century, Papa had said, with both east and west wings added in the subsequent centuries. She'd still not mastered the house's warren of rooms and passageways, and Papa said there might be more, hidden behind the plastered and paneled walls.

"Tilly."

The booming voice carried across the yard. She paused and wiped her sleeve across her brow.

"Yes, Papa."

Though it was afternoon Sir Newton Fenwick appeared at the kitchen entrance attired in his banyan, and house slippers, and the befuddled look that signaled he'd just risen from his writing desk.

At least he'd advanced no further than the cobbled path by the door. She wouldn't have to clean mud from his slippers.

"Wait there, Papa."

"I can't find the maid, Tilly. I've rung for tea and no one came. The cook has vanished as well."

At the stable door, Wulver turned, ears up, tail slapping wildly.

Sending a stick flying, she diverted the dog. Papa had aged much in the time since her mother's death. Wulver's affectionate pounce had more than once almost knocked him down. "Go back to the study, Papa. I'll be right along with your tea."

"You don't say they've run off again?"

His voice quivered with excitement. Gathering wood, she pondered how to answer. She would not indulge his superstitious phantasms and notions.

"'Twas the rain, perhaps, it being a long walk for most of them. It looks to pour even harder later tonight."

"*Humbug*," he said. "Rain is nothing to the folk in these parts, nor long walks."

She picked through the pile for the driest pieces and nudged her father into the kitchen entry, dropping the kindling and pulling off a boot.

The day's baking lay on the table, the smell tantalizing. When Wulver shot in, Tilly dove for the dog's collar.

If she could keep Wulver away, they would have plenty to eat for a day or two until she must add cookery to her list of tasks.

"Come Tilly, you are not telling me all. It was Sir Richard drove them out, was it not?"

She found a rag and wiped the dog's feet, shoving down her frustration.

"Sir Richard is dead, Papa."

"What did they say, Tilly?"

Nothing. Pressing her lips on the lie, she stroked Wulver's rough hair. The dog's undercoat had thickened. The knots and burrs would require a proper brushing, when she could spare the time.

"Honor thy father and mother, Tilly." He softened the scold with a smile.

She pulled off her other muddy boot and straightened. "Fine, Papa. They say Sir Richard appeared. Or made a noise. Or something equally ridiculous. And you need not look so gleeful. If he continues to disturb your household, if you continue to encourage that superstition, we'll not be able to keep any servants. And, dear father, I'm but one woman, and this, a big house."

"We'll send to York for some hardier folk. I have a friend in the Theosophical Society there who'll assist us."

Just what they needed: a batch of ghost-hunting servants.

"There were no crops this year, Papa, no bales of wool, no cattle. We are lucky Sir Richard died before the Crown could find him guilty of murder and treason and declare his title and estate forfeit. This myth of his haunting does us no good. We are well rid of the blackguard."

"We must trust in the Lord."

That last had been said in his Sunday morning voice. She let out another exasperated breath and stirred the fire under the still-hot kettle. It would take but a moment to steam.

"Oh, do not worry so, Tilly. I have everything in hand. There's the money from Lord Shaldon, and all those lovely sheep coming. And you've said it yourself, the land is not good for planting."

"Not in its present state. And the money from Lord Shaldon is a loan, Papa, and no good if I can't find a man to repair the stone walls of the meadow, where the sheep will be penned."

"I should have named you after that Martha who fretted about her household duties, instead of our brave queen, Matilda. Do not worry so, my dear. I'm making good progress on my book. That and the sheep will save us, you'll see."

She chewed on her lip and moved woodenly, preparing his tray.

Papa's flock at their last small parish in Cumberland had been a poor lot, the tithes undependable, requiring great economies and the occasional grant of charity dished up with a sauce of humiliation by the local squire's lady.

Mother had borne it all, right up to her death, but Tilly had seethed carrying that cross.

Papa, of course, had never noticed. For him, a story of goblins was as good as a shilling tithe, and his parishioners knew it.

When they were children, the local squire's son had been Tilly's particular friend, and she'd hoped...oh, but those had been a girl's dreams.

His mother had found him a more suitable match, and Tilly had kept her chin up while Papa officiated the couple's nuptials.

Then the letter had come informing them of this unlikely inheritance—unlikely because Papa had never heard of Sir Richard Fenwick, baronet. As Papa's potential heiress, her standing in the parish had risen more than a few notches, but she'd left Cumberland with no regrets.

And when they'd arrived at Fenwick Manor, she'd seen the truth of this rich inheritance: they'd gone from few worldly possessions to many, possessions that required a commensurate amount of money to maintain.

She shook off her glumness. Papa had been thrilled with the unexpected blessing, and so had she. To have a *chance* at a secure home and a reliable income—well, above all, she must hold on to a grateful heart. "Will you take your tray in the parlor, Papa?"

"In my library, I believe. I'm still polishing the story a local man told—"

Creak. Snick. Somewhere in the upper part of the manor, a door had swung to and closed, the sound distinctive.

CHAPTER THREE

Papa rushed to the servants' staircase, Wulver close at his heels.

"It was only the wind..."

But he'd already left. She braced herself on the table, taking in a calming breath. Papa favored opened windows and fresh air, perhaps hoping a spirit would come in on a breeze. It would only be the wind blowing a door closed, not a ghost.

Certainly not a house breaker either. They'd arrived to find the house stripped of the quality linens, silver and dishware, though no one in the neighboring village of Clampton could say who'd been brave enough to steal from a haunted house. They'd brought with them her great-aunt's few treasured pieces of silver, and the rest of their good crockery and linens had come courtesy of the Earl of Shaldon. That the earl could be so generous, considering Sir Richard's part in the murder of the previous Lady Shaldon some ten years before—well, it was another reason to be grateful.

She'd spent the few days since their arrival making Papa comfortable and hiring this lot of worthless servants, and had only begun her inventory of the household goods. Much of the furniture was broken, or rotted, and most of the trinkets and decorations were rubbish.

At least the villagers, or smugglers, or whoever had stolen from the house, had not touched the books in the ancient library.

There might be something of value somewhere in the manor, a rare hidden treasure she could sell to pay off their debt, hire proper servants, and bring in tenants with more on their mind than smuggling cargoes. If Sir Richard had been the smuggling lord in these parts, surely he had hiding places the thieves hadn't found.

She pulled out her ring of keys and fingered each of them, studying the last one. She'd matched every key to a door except this one, which didn't seem to fit anywhere.

And then of course she was missing a key to the outbuilding on the back of the hill. That was another mystery for yet another day.

Wulver wandered back into the kitchen and when the servant's bell jingled, Tilly roused herself. She'd deliver Papa's tray before the tea cooled and perhaps find time to make the rounds again. Somewhere in this house was a lock she'd missed.

Those keys.

Freddy watched, sensing the stroke of Tilly's thumb on each length of metal as she sorted them. The last and the grandest, a curlicued skeleton key, held her particular interest. And what door would that open?

When the dog entered, he held his breath. The peepholes in the kitchen cabinet were impossible to spot, but Wulver might well catch the scent of him. Since the squire's arrival, washing and shaving had been a challenge.

Thank heavens for the distracting pies cooling upon the table under a cloth. The black nose rose, and the cloth began to slide.

Freddy swallowed a chuckle. One of the bread loaves was already missing a chunk.

"*Wulver*," Tilly cried. With a sharp command and a sweep of her skirts, she hoisted the tray and ushered the beast out.

When the creaking footsteps had reached the top of the stairs, he eased the cabinet open on the hidden away hinges.

He'd discovered this covert passage early on. A convenience for him getting from attic to kitchen. Since the new squire's arrival, the secret path to the kitchens had become necessary else he'd starve. And thank goodness for the massive beast. There was only so much disappearing food one could blame on the mice or the resident cat.

He lifted the cloth and inhaled the sweet scent of fresh loaves and savory pies. The partially eaten loaf and two meat pies snuggled into his handkerchief, and from there into his pocket. With his dinner arranged, he slid out the door to the stable yard.

Between the old codger's late hours and his daughter's early ones, he'd had a devil of a time getting back into the library. Last night, in the wee hours, he'd finally had a good look at the papers upon Sir Newton's desk. And now, he had a hole in the ground to explore while he waited for the old squire to retire to his bedchamber.

In the library, Tilly poured tea and stirred in sugar and milk, watching her father across the room. Papa gripped his quill, frowning at the blotched paper spread before him.

"Before it gets cold, Papa," she chided.

He lifted his gaze and blinked.

"Your tea is ready. Do stop frowning and come. The cook managed some baking before fleeing the ghost."

"I'm lost," he said, but he set down his quill and shuffled over to join her.

"You are not lost. You are at Fenwick Manor in Yorkshire," she teased. "About to partake of a simple but ample meal, made by a better cook than the one who'll be managing tomorrow's dinner."

He blinked. "You've hired a new cook already?"

"No, Papa. I mean me."

His frown deepened. "That's false humility, daughter. Your mother taught you cookery, and she taught you well." He dug into the pie. "I've forgotten it, is all."

"Forgotten what?"

"The description of the glen. The glen where the fearsome Barghest of Troller's Gill resides, guarding a treasure."

She turned away and rolled her eyes. "Did you find Troller's Gill, then?"

Papa laughed heartily. "No, certainly not. But a gap in the earth very like, according to the man reporting it, and it is on our land. I met him at the inn after our arrival here. He took me there to the edge of it and showed me, but I hadn't brought my pencil and notebook that day."

A bead of gravy clung to his chin. She handed him a napkin.

"The description is most essential to finishing the final draft of my story. There is a fissure in the earth there, a crevice he said no one will risk exploring. And there's an ancient treasure as well. Roman or Viking gold perhaps. Or perhaps a cache left by some ancient pirate." He set down his fork. "We must go directly and have a look."

Use a setting from one of your other tall tales, she wanted to shout. "You've already visited the place, you said, and it is nigh onto dusk, and raining."

He glanced toward the window. "I didn't see it at the gloaming, which is when the fairy folk might appear. Besides, the rain has stopped."

"But the clouds have not blown through. It will start again soon."

"And dusk on a gloomy day is the best time to see supernatural creatures." He winked and shoved the last bits of pie into his mouth, chewing and swallowing rapidly, and guzzling his tea in a few quick gulps.

"Good heavens, Papa. Did you not always caution me to slow down and enjoy my meal?"

"I must hasten to dress." He pushed back his chair. "Prepare a lantern for me, will you my dear."

"But, Papa—"

"I shall be down directly. I shall bring the dog with me." He waved a hand at the tea tray. "You may stay here and tidy the kitchen."

And then he was gone.

She took in a deep breath. Papa could dress very quickly when he wished. She'd seen him rush out in the middle of the night to chase after an apparition—and in fairness, sometimes to answer a summons by a dying parishioner.

The lantern was the devil to light, and she must first get her warm shawl if she was to go out in the chill autumn evening, and go out she would. All the land hereabouts was said to be dotted with holes in the ground, bottomless caverns a man could step into and never come out of.

She shook out a napkin, covering the dishes against the manor's mice, and hurried out.

Twilight descended softly, the air thick with moisture that slicked her cheeks and glistened in the stitches of her knitted shawl. The salty air tickled her nose and carried the echoes of distant waves. They were not so far from the sea here.

"Aye, this is it." Papa rubbed his hands together, then pulled a notebook and a pencil stub from his pocket.

She'd followed him east, alternating between begging him to stay to the path and calling Wulver back from chasing the hares in the hedges.

"Please hurry, Papa. It's fair on to nightfall."

"*Gie me the hour o' gloamin' grey, It maks my heart sae cheery O, To meet thee on the lea-rig, My ain kind Dearie O.*" He laughed out loud and began to scribble.

Burns. He was quoting Robert Burns.

She fumed for long minutes, watching him. With luck once the light faded entirely, the lamp would stay lit. And if it didn't, she hoped the tinderbox in her pocket was still dry.

They'd passed a small cottage—a mere crumbling hut really—that looked abandoned. Had there been a tenant living here on a small croft? She should know that, if this truly was Papa's property.

They could stop there and dry out perhaps, or even shelter for the night. Before they left, she'd locked all the manor doors, though if any villager dared to break in and challenge the ghost—well, perhaps she should hire the brave soul.

Wulver pointed her nose east, lifted it, and froze, fur bristling, tail in the air.

The brush rustled around them. Wulver woofed, and then her tail made a tentative swish, and then beat frantically, propelling her into a man who'd stepped out of the nearby brush.

Tilly's heart leapt into her throat. It was the taller-than-herself handsome stranger she'd met by the meadow but days ago.

CHAPTER FOUR

"What the devil," Freddy cried.

Two broad paws slammed into his shoulders, and he stumbled, heart pounding wildly.

The hell-hound.

"Down, Wulver." Someone tugged at the dog. "Down, Wulver...oop."

Damn and holy hell—and for that matter, holy hell-hound. The squire was here, and his daughter, and she'd just landed upon her arse, while the beast still writhed before him spewing hot canine breath.

He poked his knee at the dog, quelling it, and reached for the lady. She was not quite as light as a flower, but her scent was, and the touch of her ungloved hand sent warmth buzzing through him.

She yanked her hand back, caught the dog by the collar and ordered it to sit.

"Are you all right, sir?" Her glance bounced over him and skittered away, her embarrassment clear. It was too dark to see whether her cheeks had gone pink, but blast it, his own were warm too.

"I didn't take the tumble, miss. Are *you* all right?"

Behind her, the squire was muttering and scribbling, oblivious to any currents buzzing between his daughter and a strange man. What was wrong with the old fool?

She smoothed her skirts. "I'm fine. So, we meet again, sir. Was that your cottage we passed on the way here?"

Here was a fine question by the daughter who was *not* a fool.

"Cottage?" He pulled a corner of bread from his pocket. The dog squirmed, its mistress hanging onto the collar.

When he crouched, she released it and the beast nosed his hand for the tidbit. He stood and scratched its neck, making it wiggle.

"She likes you."

"It's a 'she' then?" He couldn't help smiling. As children, he and his brothers had always had dogs. "That explains it, though most dogs and I rub along well together. What is your man about, here? Can I be of assistance, sir?"

The squire lifted his head and squinted.

"If you're looking for the hell-hound, sir, you have it right here."

"You know of the Barghest?"

"Heard tell of it, along with the other beasties and goblins that roam the moors." Any child growing up in the north would have been weaned on such tales.

The squire shoved his notes in his pocket and strode over—with more purpose than common sense, Freddy thought, given the terrain and the falling darkness.

"I'm Mr.—er, Sir Newton Fenwick. Must get used to that. Newly installed in Fenwick Manor.

And this is my daughter, Matilda. I'm pleased to make your acquaintance." Sir Newton snatched up his hand and pumped it. "Are you a neighbor or perhaps one of old Sir Richard's tenants?"

Bloody bad luck running into the squire and his daughter.

"Not a tenant, no, not that. How are you finding Fenwick Manor, sir?"

The older man beamed. "Delightful. I'm compiling stories of the supernatural in these parts, folklore and whatnot, to add to my chapters about Scottish and Cumberland lore. And you say you have stories?"

"I've heard a tale here or there."

"I should like to hear them. All of them." Sir Newton smiled. "I say, would you like to come and work for me?"

"I've already asked him, Father." The lady sent him a shrewd look. "I...er...spoke to him a few days ago when I was looking for men to repair the stone wall."

"Stonework?" Sir Newton shook his head. "No, no, I shall hire you to tell me your stories."

The lady's lips pressed together. Stories would not put the estate back in order, and why couldn't the old man see that?

On the other hand, sitting in the library telling stories might give him a chance to search out Sir Richard's records.

Might, but more likely Sir Newton would expect him to sit for long hours spinning yarns while he scratched away at his desk.

And the lass needed a man's help, not a storyteller's. Outdoors, he could make himself scarce whenever he pleased. Most of his searching took place at night, when the old man had vacated the library.

"I'd be better at stonework than telling stories." At least the sort of story that would interest an old vicar. Otherwise, he could have a whole officer's mess laughing with a bawdy tale, and lie like the devil when needed.

"Would you do it, then?" she asked. "We've sheep coming, and I fear they'll wander away."

"That's too big a task for one man, daughter."

"I shall go back to the village and try again. Only...if there are others, you must not tell ghost stories while you're at work, Mr....what *is* your name, sir?"

He blinked, taking her measure. The lamplight revealed a fair face scrunched into a frown that brokered no nonsense.

"Name's Freddy, miss. Freddy...Smith."

"Mr. Smith. Are you—"

"I fear you're right about those stone walls. I've seen the state of your fences and gates."

"No, no. I'll need you in the library, Mr. Smith."

Tilly turned the scowl on her father, and he bit back a grin, grateful the old man had cut off her questioning.

"No sir, I fear I can't be cooped up indoors."

"Can you tell stories outdoors?" the lady asked.

This felt like a trap. "Outdoors?"

"Papa, you can go along with Mr. Smith as he works on the wall and hear his stories. You've a need for fresh air, and the walk down to the meadow would serve you as well."

She moved quickly into negotiating wages while his head spun.

"I thank you for the offer," he said, "but—"

"Double it, Tilly," Sir Newton said.

She took in a deep breath. "Papa."

Sir Newton waved away her anxiety. "I have a bit of money and reason to believe my book will sell well, and Mr. Smith will be offering two services. You'll get your wages."

Tilly looked away and squeezed her eyes tight a moment, making him swallow a chuckle. Sir Newton was a handful to manage, and this one was the managing sort.

"The book selling well would be good luck for you, sir," he said.

"'Tis said also that there might be things of value at Fenwick Manor, if we can but find them. The Fenwicks were Papists for a time. When I inherited, an old friend wrote to me about the family history. Hidden away at the Manor were the usual gold candlesticks, crucifix, and communion cup. Some of those were found and sold in the last century. But I've heard a tale that there ought to have been more of them as well as a medieval bible."

"And please don't forget Sir Richard's hidden smuggling treasure." Tilly said. "And the Viking gold buried inside this fissure. All there for the taking."

Her father beamed, ignoring—or not noticing her sarcasm. "Yes, yes. So many treasures. If someone can find them, they may share in the spoils."

"The shadows are falling. Mr. Smith. Will double my previous offer suffice? And my father will come out and hear your stories and perhaps shift a stone or two when needed. What say you?"

He was trapped, well and good.

"Please."

He heard the edge of desperation in her voice, much like her plaintive appeal to the servants he'd driven away, and guilt gnawed at him again.

He touched a hand to his forehead, in a poor salute that would have brought a dressing down from his Major. "We may as well start tomorrow then, miss."

"Thank you." She bestowed him a smile that almost made this foolish distraction worthwhile. "I'll meet you in the stable yard tomorrow morning and show you—"

"*I'll* meet you, Mr. Smith," Sir Newton said.

He sighed. "I'll start myself. I know which walls you're speaking of. You'll find me there, Sir Newton, and good night to you both. Mind your steps here, so you don't take another tumble."

He escaped into the night.

"My father will bring you breakfast," the lady called.

He chuckled to himself. He had breakfast in his pocket, but if she wanted to feed him again, he might as well eat this last pie.

He'd eat better, he'd still have the night to search, and maybe between stories, he could find out from Sir Newton where the old squire kept his important papers.

It was full dark by the time they reached the Manor, Tilly stumbling all the way over holes and trying not to drag her father down with her. All she wanted was her bed and to rest her sore muscles before the busy day ahead—and well, until she'd hired proper staff, every day ahead would be busy enough to make every muscle even sorer, wouldn't it?

In the stable yard, Wulver paused and growled.

CHAPTER FIVE

A man emerged from the shadows, his dark coat absorbing the lamplight. Anxiety threaded through her, but Papa, being used to seeing ghouls and goblins in the dark, must have recognized him because he called out a greeting.

Wulver wasn't having it though. She hovered near Tilly and commenced a menacing rumbling.

"Mr. Greggson, isn't it?" Papa shook the visitor's hand.

When the man moved into the light, his gaze raked her, raising her own urge to growl.

"I was in the area and thought I'd call," he said. "None of the servants were about."

Papa paused and rubbed his chin. "Yes, yes. Perhaps you'd like to come in and, er, join us for a bit of cold supper. My dear, would you run along and—"

"I'll put the kettle on and bring up a tray."

"Excellent," Papa said, "We'll be in the parlor."

Tilly hurried to unlock the kitchen door, tugging a stiff Wulver along with her. She couldn't account for their clear discomfort—hers, the dog's, and surprisingly, her father's. Papa hadn't introduced her to this late caller, Mr. Greggson, whoever he might be. And he wasn't taking the man to his library, which was where he'd entertained the local innkeeper when he'd called.

She lit more lamps, stirred the fire, and heard the men shuffle in and proceed directly through the kitchen to the stairs. Wulver pattered off after them.

The dog would normally have stayed close to the food.

Tilly hastily assembled a tray, adding an extra cup, in case she might be invited to stay.

Well, she would stay anyway, invited or not. She was hostess of a great manor house now and her affable father was uncomfortable with this visitor, as was her dog who was an excellent judge of character.

Wulver's endorsement of Freddy Smith—now there was a false name if ever she'd heard one— had reinforced her own instincts. He'd been quite kind to Papa, and quite sturdy in weathering Wulver's pounce, and so strong helping her to her feet...

A shiver went through her, an echo of the tingle she'd felt gripping his hand, a feeling she'd never encountered, not that she'd ever been properly courted.

Have a care, Tilly. He was handsome, all right, but a stranger.

Still, working outside in the open field, how could he do them harm? And Papa would be there getting fresh air, and maybe even shifting a few small stones.

While he was out listening to Freddy's tales, she could take a few moments between household chores to search out papers that might show her where to find the lock that matched the last key on her ring.

And perhaps...perhaps the key would lead her to something of value. A cache of pounds sterling would be her first choice, but the medieval bible Papa mentioned would be lovely. Surely such an ancient book would be wonderfully illuminated and in Latin she might be able to decipher. Or... they could put it up immediately for auction, in London perhaps, or Oxford. Certainly, they must do so, unless they found the smuggler's treasure, or Papa's yet-to-be-finished tome on folklore sold well.

She shook off this particular set of worries and hefted her tray.

Papa had lit a lamp, the only light illuminating the shabby table's decanter of brandy.

"Here you go, gentlemen," she said, placing the tray on the table.

Papa thanked her, and strangely for him, said no more. She would definitely stay.

"Sitting in the dark." She *tsked* and moved to light a nearby branch of candles.

There were no other tapers here, but at least the new light allowed her a better assessment of their visitor. Mr. Greggson was a youngish man, a gentleman, with blond good looks. He likely was not much older than her own twenty-five years. Handsome, in a lean, cultivated way, many women might find him better-looking than the powerfully built, rougher-hewn Freddy Smith. Not her though. She sensed Greggson was no gentleman, in all the ways that mattered.

And she didn't like him at all.

"My dear." Papa had perhaps finally realized she intended to stay. "Mr. Greggson is the local

Riding Officer. Greggson, this is my daughter Miss Fenwick."

They exchanged polite greetings, and Tilly poured tea and took an empty chair in the shadows. Wulver plopped down next to her.

Papa inquired about the local smuggling, and Greggson recounted a story of a recent arrest up the coast near Whitby, so vague as to seem made up. When Papa failed to probe, the conversation lagged.

She ought to stay quiet and listen, but it wasn't in her nature. "What brings the local Riding Officer to Fenwick Manor on this moonless night? I assure you my father and I have our hands full settling in here. We are not engaged in smuggling, nor do we ever contemplate taking up the free trade."

Greggson's soft chuckle slithered along her skin. "I'm happy to hear that, Miss Fenwick. Though I suspect you might have tenants, or others, who will take advantage of the late Sir Richard's storerooms."

"Apparently not. Every cubbyhole at Fenwick Manor appears to be haunted."

He scoffed. "Is that why you've no servants on duty? Ghosts are keeping them away?"

She glanced at her father. He was studying his brandy, seemingly preoccupied.

"Fenwick Manor is a large house requiring a great deal of work. And I am a clergyman's daughter, used to hard work and expecting it of others. Not everyone is willing to labor under those terms."

"Perhaps I could offer my assistance. I know of a woman who might serve as housekeeper."

Papa's head shot up. He'd been listening all along, and this proposal didn't please him.

Perhaps Greggson associated with women who were less than respectable.

"No, no," she demurred, crossing her fingers in her lap. "I have the matter quite in hand, sir."

"My daughter is right," Papa said, "though it is most kind of you, most kind indeed. In any case, Lord Farnsworth from the Home Office visited us the day we arrived here and assured us of his help and support. Friend of Lord Shaldon, he is. Has some business in this area. The government intends to continue to address the more violent of the gangs hereabouts." Papa eyed his glass again. "Though I suppose you are aware of that, considering your position."

Greggson twirled his brandy, watching it catch the light. "That is why I'm here, Sir Newton. And I hope you'll inform me of any suspicious activities you come across." A long pause followed as his eyes narrowed. "There is one man in particular rumored to have been seen in these parts recently."

"What man is that?" Papa asked.

Tilly's heart thumped, and she held her breath.

"The name is Sandford or some such, I believe. The criminal sort, from the Durham area. Sir Richard's death creates a vacuum that will want filling."

"I don't recognize that name. Do you, my dear?"

"No. What does this criminal sort look like?"

"Dark, they say, and about your father's height."

Papa was a tall man. As was Freddy Smith.

In a country where a man could be hanged for stealing food, any hungry man might be the criminal sort. One might have a morally sound reason to go from being a Sandford to a Smith.

Who was this Mr. Greggson, paying a call so late in the evening to pry? Never mind her own instincts about the appealing Mr. Freddy Smith; her dog had approved of him, and Wulver's judgment had never erred.

"How alarming." Her voice shook, and she paused for a breath. Greggson wouldn't know her shakiness was anger, not fear. Let him think her a timid ninny. "What crimes has this Mr. Sandford committed?"

"He's run a smuggling enterprise, a violent one. Word is that he's not averse to committing murder."

Whose word?

She took another deep breath, getting herself under control. As a clergyman's daughter, she was forever having to temper her inclination to say what she really thought.

"Goodness," was all she could manage.

"A serious charge," Papa said, rising. "Well, as my daughter says, the night is moonless, and with such dangerous types rumored to be in the area, you'll want to be on your way, Mr. Greggson."

Greggson rose and smiled at Tilly, his gaze level with hers. "Will you light my way out, Miss Fenwick?"

"I shall accompany you," Papa said. "If you would see to the tray, my dear."

Greggson smirked at her father's back, and he would have come to her side, but Wulver blocked him.

"Come along, Mr. Greggson," Papa said.

Tilly nodded. "Go with them, Wulver."

CHAPTER SIX

Juggling her tray and her candle, she arrived in the kitchen and found Papa ushering in Wulver, shaking his head. "He's off and away."

"I hope he doesn't make many such evening calls. Did you lock the door, Papa?"

While she busied herself with the dishes, her father shuffled back to the entryway and returned a few moments later, frowning.

For the first time since they'd arrived, she felt a moment of apprehension, unrelated to money or supernatural creatures. They were all alone, the two of them, in a large manor house, on the Yorkshire coast, and tonight they'd encountered two flesh and blood men, both of questionable backgrounds.

"Shall we write to your colleague in York for servants?" The house, once occupied by staff, would feel far less eerie, especially on nights such as this.

"You'll tell me if Captain Greggson seeks you out," Papa said.

Dread slithered through her, making her shiver. What had the man said to Papa as he was leaving?

Nothing, probably. He'd said it all in that one request that she be the one to light his way out.

The late cup of tea roiled in her stomach and threatened to come up. Papa's property wasn't entailed. When they'd stopped for a few days in York, he'd seen both a physician and a solicitor. Now that he was a man of property, he'd written a proper will, making her his sole heir.

"Yes, of course," she said.

And then, to distract him from worry she added, "I'll do the same if Freddy Smith seeks me out."

He grunted and broke off a corner of a pie, nibbling on it. "I had a good feeling about Freddy Smith." He rubbed his stomach. "You must get this cook back. Wrap up these pasties well and bring them along for breakfast tomorrow. The boy will be hungry when we start on the fence."

There *was* something boyish about Freddy, but his broad shoulders and dark stubble were those of a full-grown man, and well Papa knew it.

"He'll want more than meals, Papa. What of the items of value we might uncover here, including the bible? Perhaps I should search while you work with him in the field, so we can raise enough money for his double wages. After I hire back the cook."

"You must not worry so, Tilly."

"Perhaps more double wages and a few prayers of, *er*, exorcism will convince the other servants to come back. I found a copy of the *Roman Rituale* among the Latin histories."

Papa laughed. "The archbishop would love to hear of me performing a Papist rite. Do not worry, oh ye of little faith. Your papa has all well in hand."

The next morning, escorted by Wulver, Papa went off with the food, whilst she saw to their two horses and then walked off to the village to find the cook he had admired so. After the previous night's rain, the day had bloomed fair, an autumn day filled with sunshine and cool breezes.

By midday, she had returned with Sir Richard's old cook, Rose, who brought her grandson with her to work as a kitchen boy, and also helped convince Edie, a former housemaid at Fenwick Manor, to agree to a trial as housekeeper. The cook had even persuaded Max, the stable lad who'd run away to come back.

Rose and Edie declined to reside in the manor house, but they were happy to work for the increased wages Tilly had offered. Max, after some small bullying and a promise to keep Wulver from pouncing on him, agreed to bunk in the stables—also for more wages.

Papa *would* see how much faith Tilly could muster when needed. If they couldn't discover a hidden treasure, if Papa couldn't finish his book, then Lord Shaldon must stake them for another loan.

On her way to the village, she'd found Freddy hard at work on the stone fence, Papa scribbling away on his notes. When she'd finally settled her new staff and returned to visit the two men, they'd moved down the slope toward the thicket of trees that bordered a stream she could hear but not see. Papa had shed his coat and rolled up his sleeves, and he was working alongside Freddy, laughing at something the younger man said, the rare autumn sun lighting his face.

Both men, in fact, had rolled up their sleeves. Corded muscles flexed as Freddy hefted a large stone into place, making her suddenly light-headed.

His gaze met hers and his mouth quirked in a wry smile, setting her insides to dancing.

Freddy had sensed her arrival even before she'd come round the bend, his pulse quickening with anticipation. When her gaze landed on him, her smile faded and her eyes darkened to midnight blue.

Fair along to being smitten by the squire's daughter, he was, and wasn't that a laugh? Well it would be, if he didn't have his brother and his mother to see to. Finding the proof of Sir Richard's bribes, bringing his brother back, that's what he needed to be about, not building a fence for sheep or yearning after a lady.

But blast it, she was lovely, and the squire seemed a righteous man. How righteous, he couldn't be sure, and he wouldn't risk asking for help. Not until he had proof in his hands.

"It's a fine piece of work you've done this day." The lovely lass had been as tongue-tied for a moment as himself, but she'd finally caught her breath. She looked away, fondling the scruff of the dog who'd leaned up against her. The lucky beast.

And now he was jealous of a dog. He swallowed a laugh.

"Aye," Sir Newton said, "in all ways. Freddy has imparted a delicious story of hobgoblins that lived in the bog near his home and snatched children."

"That sounds more frightening than delicious." Her voice quivered, and she cleared her throat, putting on a serious face. "But you've almost finished this broken wall. I believe if the sheep appear tomorrow, I won't worry so about them."

"Then I'll collect my double wages and be on my way," he teased.

She blinked, her color rising. "After only one story? Papa, how many do you require before Mr. Smith is free to go?"

The dog lifted her nose in the air and froze.

The skin at his nape quivered. Wulver was an intelligent beast, and he was a man who'd learned to heed warnings no matter how they arrived.

He'd made more than one trip that day down the hill to the burn, fetching them water. Now was a good time to go again.

"I'll dip a fresh pitcher." He snatched up his coat and the urn heading down the slope and vaulting the stone wall.

"But I'd be happy to..." Tilly's words cut off as he disappeared into the tree line.

When he'd reached a dense thicket, he paused and peered through a thatch of evergreen. The lass and her father had turned and were watching a horse and its rider come into view.

Basil Greggson, bold as life, coming around to the back of the manor instead of up the drive to the main door.

Aye, he'd seen Greggson plenty of times on the manor grounds. Before the new squire's arrival, he'd seen the bastard inside the manor house sneaking up the stairs and into the library, and it had been a near thing ducking out of the Riding Officer's way.

He'd seen and heard Greggson last night as well. The route to the attic passed by the parlor and dining room. He'd observed the visit through one of the manor's peepholes.

Greggson was a fraud, as thick as any of Sir Richard's other thieves.

It had seemed a fool's errand to search Fenwick Manor, but his mother had sworn the solicitor she'd paid said Sir Richard had records hidden that might help bring his brother home. Freddy had set off making inquiries along the coast, working his way south to the manor. Greggson might have heard a man was asking about him, might have guessed a connection to the man transported.

Considering Greggson's exploration of the library, maybe the solicitor had been right. Maybe something at Fenwick Manor would implicate Greggson.

After searching, the Riding Officer had left empty handed. If there was evidence here, Freddy would find it—ledgers, notes, papers, whatever items the earl's men overlooked when they captured Sir Richard because they weren't thinking of the John Black who'd been unjustly transported.

Greggson reined in his horse and greeted the Squire and his daughter from the saddle. Neither the old man nor Tilly showed the deference of a bow or a curtsy, and good for them. Tilly had a hand on her dog restraining the beast. She was a strong lass, built of iron and good sense. He'd wager she was not a bit fooled by the mounted bastard.

The breeze carried snippets of conversation Freddy's way. Greggson gestured at the low stone wall. "...all by yourself," he said.

"Old, I am, but hardy..." The breeze swallowed Sir Newton's words and rattled the damp turning leaves from the trees. Aye, but this had been a stormy autumn, with more rain to come.

He held his breath and watched Tilly shake her head, her mouth shaping the word "no."

Scowling, she let loose of the dog and trudged over to the wall for Sir Newton's coat while the two men continued talking, the words inaudible.

"It's growing too cool for you to stand around chatting, Father." Tilly's voice carried loudly, as though she were talking to a man hard of hearing.

Or one hiding in the trees.

"Shall we gather our things and wish Mr. Greggson a good day?"

Sir Newton took the coat and slipped it on. They were going home. The day's work was done.

She tossed the two cups into the basket.

Greggson's face screwed up in a frown. "You put your daughter to work on the stone wall?"

Sir Newton smiled as he buttoned his coat. "You must not repeat that tale in the village."

He let out a breath. The old vicar wouldn't lie, but he wouldn't give Freddy away either, and that made his hair rise again. Sir Newton might be something more than a daft chaser of fairy tales.

"There is no shame in hard work, isn't that right, Father?"

The old man clasped her hand and looked up to the sky. "No indeed, for as St. Paul said, 'in labor and toil, we worked night and day'."

Freddy choked. The old vicar's Sunday voice carried easily into the trees.

"The work of the hand feeds the work of the mind, and I shall go back to my manuscript, my muse renewed by fresh air and physical labor. Be off with you, Mr. Greggson." The last was said with joviality, and as the Riding Officer turned his horse away, Sir Newton cast a look back at the burn and winked.

Freddy sidled silently down the hill, as careful to avoid snapping a twig as he'd been in the wilds of Canada.

Sir Newton had not revealed him, nor had his daughter.

Did they distrust the Riding Officer more than himself? Or did they know more about himself than they were letting on?

No. No, it couldn't be that last. They hadn't a clue who he was, what he was about, or where he was living.

Behind him a branch rustled, and he slid into a shadow.

"Now where is that pitcher, Wulver?"

The beast burst through the shrubs and its owner soon followed. Sunlight trickled through the trees and dappled her cheeks, showing her high color.

He lifted the urn. "Still haven't filled it."

She took it from him and gazed up at him, her face serious. "Where do you live, Mr. Smith?"

No, he had the right of it. Neither Tilly nor Sir Newton knew who he was or where he lived.

"I'm near the village, miss."

She frowned. "Do you live in that tumble-down cottage we passed on the way to the glen? I asked you last night, but you never answered my question."

What should he answer? Saying yes would be easy, but he wouldn't put it past this bold lass to investigate the lie. "No," he said.

"Who *are* you, Freddy Smith?"

"I'm but a countryman, fallen on hard times."

She raised an eyebrow. "I've never seen anyone scamper off so adroitly as you just did. Are you a smuggler?"

"No, miss."

"A poacher?"

"No. I told you that the day we met."

Her eyes narrowed on him, glinting blue inside the fringe of dark lashes. "You're most certainly a smuggler if you're dodging the Riding Officer."

"No." Not now, anyway, and as a lad at home, he'd only taken part on the rare occasion when the local fellows needed a hand. "I really was intending to fetch more water."

"Without making a sound."

"I was once a soldier, miss. I learned to move quietly then."

She cocked her head. "Were you with Wellington at Waterloo?"

He'd missed that battle, but only because he was halfway around the world when Napoleon resurfaced. "No. I was in the Low Countries, then in Ireland for a time, and then Canada for a spell."

"And you were discharged?"

"I..." he took a deep breath. "I sold out."

Her mouth dropped. "You were an officer?" She nodded. "Yes. Of course."

Of course, what? Blast him for his damnable pride, he'd slipped. He'd taken great pains to fit in here as a working man. He should have let her believe he was one of the unwashed footslogs sent home when the wars were over.

"What do you know about this Mr. Greggson?"

He held her gaze, studying her right back, pleasure churning in him as her color rose. Dark hair had slipped from under that brown bonnet that framed full lips, pink cheeks, and eyes as blue as a clear evening sky. If she were his, she'd never wear a bonnet that ugly. Why ever had no man snatched her up?

Aye, well, it was no doubt her duty to her father and her past lack of wealth that had kept her from the marriage bed, and it was her abounding good sense that kept her out of the other sort of trouble with men.

"Greggson is corrupt." Speaking so boldly was risky, but he'd be damned if he'd let this lass stumble into trouble with the Riding Officer. "Were you my sister or my sweetheart, I'd tell you to steer clear of him."

Her eyes widened. "There's no reason for him to molest me. I have no money, no prospects for more than this poor bit of land and ramshackle manor."

"I beg your pardon, miss, but I'll dare to speak boldly because you are no fool. This land and this manor are not insubstantial, but even if they were, the average man doesn't need the prospect of money or property to try his hand at a lovely young woman like yourself."

The high color in her cheeks deepened, and she pressed her lips together as if doing so would drive the blood back to where it belonged.

"I wish you good day then." Heart pounding, he rushed off down to the burn, tempted to plunge into the bracing cold water and remind himself he was better than the average man. He'd been an officer, and he was still a gentleman, and he didn't try his hand at innocent virgins even those past the first bloom of girlhood.

And what an idiot he was.

Tilly clutched the pitcher, its handle still warm from his hand, and watched him disappear. She could follow him and see where he lived.

Hot blood rushed her again. That way lay danger, and stumbling into that danger would be foolish, with Papa needing her, with Fenwick Manor needing so much care. And Freddy was right—she wasn't a fool.

Perhaps *he* was though, if he thought she was lovely.

She picked her way up the embankment, following the stone fence to the far corner. Papa had gone ahead, anticipating a taste of the new cook's baking. He'd go straight from the kitchen to his library and commence his writing, eating dinner from a tray.

At the far corner where the hedges began, she coaxed Wulver over and hefted her skirts, climbing the stile onto the path near the low narrow building where she'd first met Freddy Smith.

Was this one of the hiding places for Sir Richard's smuggled goods? If so, the key was lost. She'd come back tomorrow with an axe.

How many more secret doors and lost keys were there at Fenwick Manor? She'd been through every storeroom and outbuilding she could find—except this one, which was far too small to hold barrels or crates.

Though it had been built into a low hill in the back of the manor house, under the oldest part of the structure, so perhaps it spilled into a cave or cellar.

Except, she'd explored, and the cellars had no passages leading this way. She was being fanciful. This was probably an old well house.

The cook and Edie had worked here before. She would ask them.

As she started up the hill, she heard a rustle behind her and for a fleeting moment, hoped that it was Freddy Smith.

But Wulver growled and her spine tingled. Greggson had come back.

CHAPTER SEVEN

"Do not tell me you were really working on the stone wall with your father," Mr. Greggson called.

He dismounted and approached, leading his horse. Wulver's hair bristled, and her growl was a low buzzing like a bee swarm threatening to strike.

"Damnation." He halted and held out his hand. "Your dog is protective."

"Yes. Isn't she lovely?"

He smirked. "*She? What* is she?"

"She's the loveliest parts of this or that breed."

"Newfoundland, perhaps," he said. "Or Wolfhound."

"Perhaps, but Papa named her Wulver for the werewolf of the Shetland Isles. She might also be part Hound of Hell."

Greggson smiled.

Flashing his straight teeth might work well on a green girl, but a plain woman like herself, who'd stood on the sidelines and watched all the love affairs in the parish play out, a woman like her could see it was only his lips lifting up at the corners.

"She has a lovely white streak where she was struck by devil's lightning as a pup," she said. "Or perhaps it was her mother that was struck when Wulver was in the womb. I always forget what the gypsy woman told me."

His laugh was a false strangled noise. "Now you are spinning me a tale, Miss Fenwick."

She shrugged. Papa had always been kind to the Romany passing through. If he chose not to believe she'd consulted them, so be it, but he could keep his hands away from her dog. "I wish you a good day. Please do let my father know if you have business on Fenwick Manor. He would like to be informed if his tenants are free-trading."

The cloud-covered sun had surely slipped lower. Dusk came quickly at this time of the year, and two men had told her to not be alone with this man.

"Come along, Wulver." She strode off toward the manor house, and, sensing the absence of the dog, she turned to look.

Greggson stood locking eyes with the dog in a duel of mutual loathing.

"Mr. Greggson," she called. "I believe she does not like you either. Let us call a truce and go our separate ways. Come, Wulver."

The dog hesitated and finally came.

Freddy watched from the shadows again.

Three times in the past twenty-four hours, Greggson had appeared at Fenwick Manor. He was nervous as well about a man making inquiries, and a nervous villain might turn dangerous.

Greggson had his cutlass and his pistols well within reach and whether or not Tilly knew it, her dog had been in peril.

And Tilly's impertinent talk put her in peril as well. A man like Greggson expected deference, especially from women.

Well, and he liked a bit of deference himself, but respect was earned, not bestowed, a truth drilled into him as a boy. The lesson had been invaluable for an officer leading rabble and ruffians into battle.

Tilly cleared the top of the hill, and Greggson mounted and rode away. He waited longer and then used his key on the door of the outbuilding, pondering the Riding Officer.

Freddy had never used his real name in his inquiries. Greggson's mention of the name Sandford had been him fishing to see if the squire knew the name of the man transported. Sir Newton had shown no reaction.

He'd best get to the business of probing the new squire. Sir Newton might truly be more than a dreamy old scribbler.

Before Tilly could make her way to the library to see what Papa wanted on his dinner tray, he sought her out in her bedchamber where she'd gone to deposit her heavy shawl.

"Lord Farnsworth called while we were out," he said. "I wish he had come around to the field where we were working. I did so wish to speak with him."

Papa blinked, his gaze traveling around the dark room. "Good heavens. We must refurbish this chamber for you, Tilly. It's hardly a room for a young woman. You need new hangings and curtains, something bright and cheerful. Your mother was always partial to yellow. Even on cloudy days, it brought in the sun, she always said."

"I remember, and that will be lovely, Papa." And a trip to the drapers would be delayed, as long as they were paying servants double wages. "Until then, this is fine for me."

It was the third most respectable chamber in the house, her father's being the second best.

Both were smaller than the grand bedchamber where Sir Richard had been shot. Not even Papa could bear the ghosts of the room where generations of Fenwick baronets had slept.

"Shall we expect Lord Farnsworth to return?" she asked, "Or shall you call on him tomorrow?"

He tipped his head. "Yes. Yes, perhaps I shall call upon him tomorrow. He's lodging at Gorse Point Cottage."

"Yes, you told me. But what of the stone wall and your stories?"

He rubbed his belly. "The new cook seems to have a fine way with a pudding. What do you think if we invite Farnsworth for dinner tomorrow night?" he asked. "Can we put on a feast for him?"

They'd arrived to find Sir Richard's larder emptied, all to be expected, she supposed. Not even a ghost could keep hungry people away from food, and why should the villagers starve while the mice feasted?

"There's perch in the stream, they say, and somewhere I'll find a good joint of beef or a ham, and fowl. I shall talk to the cook. We can lay out three courses at least."

He kissed her forehead. "You're a good girl. But who will we have to serve them?"

"I'll have Edie, the new housekeeper, lend a hand with the service."

"Perhaps...what about Freddy Smith? He seems a respectable sort. Clean, for a man living who-knows-where, and well-spoken. Intelligent, too. Brush the dust off his coats and put a pair of white gloves on him, perhaps he'd make a suitable footman." He took in a sharp breath. "Or butler. Shall I ask him?"

Freddy Smith as footman or butler, underfoot all the day? The thought sent a thrill through her, one that she must squelch.

"He seems the proud sort, Papa." Did her father know Freddy had been an officer who'd had the wherewithal to buy a commission?

That was Freddy's secret to tell. "I'm not sure we'll need a butler any time soon. Let me deal with him." She took his elbow and led him to the door. "I must go now and talk to Edie and Rose."

She found Edie in the old wing of the house, duster in hand, staring at the ornately carved door of the late Sir Richard's bedchamber.

"Edie," she said.

The girl started and her face settled into her usual frown. "What do you plan to do with that room?" she asked.

"Why? Because it's haunted? I don't believe in ghosts."

Edie shook her head. "Nor do I. But..."

Tilly sighed. "But Sir Richard was so very bad." Impulsively, she turned the latch on the door and pushed it open. "Let's have a look." She stepped in and pinched her nose, holding her breath.

The room smelled of mildew and ancient wood, but worse was the sensation of the air being sucked from her.

She'd seen this chamber on her tour of the house, and then again when choosing their bedchambers. Sir Richard's lair had been stripped of bloodied hangings and the bullet holes repaired, and yet it still managed to set her head spinning. Each time, she'd walked into this same suffocating, invisible cloud.

Ghosts didn't exist, but good and evil—that she believed in. Sir Richard had certainly lived in the presence of evil, had certainly done evil deeds.

Edie crossed the room and began to struggle with the window. She hastened to help, and they pounded and shoved until the pane of glass swung freely. They both took great gulps of the moist air.

"I used to clean this room," Edie said. "Me and another girl would work like whirlwinds, trying to finish before the Squire came. We'd hear him bellowin' in the hall and stompin' up the stairs and we'd gather our rags and brooms and make for the panel."

"The panel?"

Edie waved a hand toward the paneled wall flanking the fireplace. "The secret door. Or, not so secret, really."

"Show me."

Edie led her to the paneling. Wood trim formed rectangles along seamed panels of oak, darkened by years of smoke and oiling. Even the wood held a dank, musty smell.

"It all looks alike, don't it?" Edie said. "But here." She pushed on a wooden medallion, and a group of panels, the size of a door clicked and popped open.

"Good heavens," Tilly said. Inside was darkness. She yanked the opening wider and peered in. A stark dingy-walled corridor, led off past the fireplace.

The skin on her neck rippled. "Does each bedchamber have an entry like this?"

"No. At least, not as I know of. Only this one and the parlor and dining room, but 'tis said the Fenwicks were once Papists. Some say the walls hold the bones of those who couldn't get out when the Roundheads came."

The existence of priest holes, she could believe, but of priest holes filled with old bones? The thought gave her goosebumps.

She took a deep breath. "What do you say, Edie?"

The young woman shrugged. "This one leads to the corridor, and there be no bones here. But if there be bones elsewhere, we ought to give them a proper burial."

She nodded. "That would be the Christian way." She closed the panel door. "Will you take me on a tour and show me what you know, tomorrow...or, drat, not tomorrow. My father wants to host a dinner tomorrow. Come, let's talk to Rose. I'll need both your help."

In the kitchen they found Rose tidying up. Her grandson pushed a broom around while another boy held a mop, both of them laughing hysterically and bedeviling a grumbling Wulver, who was feinting, springing up, and attacking each weapon in turn.

"That's enough," Rose said. "Leave the poor beast be."

The dog wriggled her great bulk and went to nose each of the boys.

"I'm sorry, miss," Rose said. "You boys should know that even a good-natured dog can have enough."

"Aye, if she bites you, Pip," Edie said, "you'll have got what you deserve."

"She won't bite me, Edie," the boy called Pip said. "Why look here." He put a grimy hand between Wulver's jaws and laughed as the dog mouthed it.

"You're a brave one, Pip," Tilly said. "Have you come seeking work?"

"He's my cousin," Edie said, "and he's come to sneak around looking for the ghost and to fetch me home."

"Could you run a message from Sir Newton to Gorse Point Cottage? No, that is probably too far for you to walk so late in the day."

"Not that it's too far," Edie said, "but we don't let Pip out and about on his own much after dusk."

The boy's brow furrowed suddenly. Edie had just reminded him of something that frightened him. What dangers had the boy encountered?

She'd let it be. "Come along with Edie tomorrow, Pip, and I'll have work for you," Tilly said. "And please, spread the word that my dog is a good-tempered beast, not at all a hell-hound. Now, Rose, where are the biscuits you made for the squire? Boys, you may have some while Rose and Edie and I plan tomorrow night's dinner."

The next morning, she sent her father off early on one of the horses, congratulating herself that for two days in a row he'd got himself out of his dressing gown and away from his desk. The fresh air would do him good, and visiting a neighbor, a sensible friend to the great Earl of Shaldon, was the best sort of medicine for a fanciful man.

Plans for the evening's dinner were well underway. Edie had set about readying the linens, and table settings, the cook had arrived that morning with more provisions and had begun her baking, and she herself would procure the rest of the fare they would need.

And hopefully a footman.

She stepped out of the kitchen into the yard.

Pip was there, laughing, running in circles with Wulver right on his heels.

"Did you find everything?" she called.

He waved, said something to the dog, and picked up a clutch of fishing rods. She shifted her own two large baskets and closed the door behind her.

"Wulver, you stay," she said.

"Can she not go with us, miss? We'll be safer."

"Are you worried, walking with me in the daylight? Though I can see we'll not have much of that with these clouds. It will rain again today, if not this afternoon, then later tonight. We'd best make quick work of our task."

Wulver plopped at her feet, shifting from side to side.

"Oh, very well, but you must keep her out of our baskets, Pip."

They found Freddy in the field, already at work.

He lifted his cap a quarter inch, wished her a good morning, and patted the dog. "And where is my colleague?" he asked. "Have you replaced him with this pint-sized mason? You'll not be demanding a ghost story, will you?" he asked the boy.

Pip's eyes went wide. "Have you seen the ghost, sir?"

The two didn't know each other. Who was Freddy Smith, really? Where had he come from?

"This is Pip. Pip, this is Mr. Smith. And my father has gone to pay a call at Gorse Point Cottage. I fear there won't be much work on the wall today. Do you know how to fish, Mr. Smith?"

CHAPTER EIGHT

Freddy positioned a stone into the wall, eyeing the lass, trying to catch up. She'd crammed a few interesting tidbits into that one sentence.

So, Pip must be one of the local folk, the folk he'd been dodging since his arrival at Fenwick Manor. He'd done his investigating elsewhere, and except one afternoon spent in the taproom of Scruggs's inn, he'd mostly avoided the village of Clampton. Passing through hamlets and towns, he'd learned that Greggson was known, and hated from Whitby to Scarborough. He'd not even had to pay to get men to talk. Here, though, people would be nosy about fresh folk like himself, a matter of survival, seeing who was moving into their parish.

And if Sir Newton was off paying a call at Gorse Point Cottage, 'twas one of the Earl of Shaldon's men who'd arrived there, not the Earl's daughter who would be taking possession of the estate. Unless the Earl himself had come.

Had the Earl called on the Squire? If Shaldon or one of his men was here, he'd need to finish this business sooner rather than later. He wasn't at all sure the Earl's men would be allies.

And what was that last bit? She wanted to know if he knew how to fish?

"Every respectable Englishman knows how to fish," he said.

Her lips quirked. "Well then, as I surmise that you're probably respectable, I should very much like it if you would assist young Pip here with his line, perhaps drop one of your own. Father is having a guest for dinner tonight, and I'd like a few good fish for our meal. I've told Pip he may take home all the extra he's caught, and if you catch enough, you may have some for yourself, as well."

He raised an eyebrow. "In lieu of my wages?"

She laughed, and her face lit, making her bloom from pretty to beautiful. "You've done the work of two men already. You shall have your wages." She picked up her baskets. "Somehow. Come along then."

He followed her down to the stream, as the barking dog and laughing boy ran ahead, crashing through the brush, sending a warm rush of memories through him.

He'd had happy days like this with his two brothers, school holidays when they'd go off fishing and running wild near their own country manor.

His middle brother was gone in the war. He must bring the youngest one home before it was too late. Spending his time building walls and fishing wouldn't help.

And yet... Tilly and Sir Newton might be folk who would help him.

"Right here," Pip said.

Tilly turned an inquiring look his way, deferring to his judgment, lighting a tingle of pride in him.

Good God. He'd long ago put aside tingles over maidens.

"Aye, you've chosen well," he said. "Let's get you set up."

As he helped the boy with his rod, he glanced up and saw her approving gaze. She knew a fair bit about fishing herself, he suspected.

"Shall I set you up with a line also, Miss Fenwick?" he asked, stepping back to join her.

She bit her lip. "No. That is, not today." She took a deep breath and faced him. "I must ask another service of you, if you are willing."

Heat flared in him, and he held himself still. Surely she wouldn't be asking that sort of service of him.

"Lord Farnsworth is at Gorse Point Cottage. Father has invited him for dinner tonight. Father wanted to know...he wanted to hire you to aid with the service tonight, as a...a footman."

"A footman."

Lord Farnsworth was coming to dinner. He was one of the secretive men from the Home Office thick as thieves with the Earl of Shaldon. And whether any of them had a role in his brother's undoing, he wasn't sure.

Nor was he sure whether he wished to be so openly serving the man's dinner. Stealth and secrecy had seemed a good idea when he'd arrived at the deserted manor.

"Lord Farnsworth is an associate of Lord Shaldon, who has been quite helpful to us," Tilly said. "Father wishes to make a good show of it."

He'd been searching for days with no success. He could easily play a footman and perhaps he'd learn something from the conversation.

Tilly screwed up her mouth and shook her head. "No, I do apologize. I know you are not what you seem, and it would be lowering—"

"I'll do it." He'd be able to hear their conversation directly, standing at their elbows, instead of garbled through a panel of wood.

"Oh," she said.

"Miss," the boy called. The lad had braced his heels and was struggling mightily.

"Hold there, Pip," he called.

It seemed only a short while later when Tilly packed the last fish away. Freddy Smith was indeed more than he seemed: kind to the boy and the dog, firm with both of them, and where she was concerned...goodness, she must get hold of herself.

She lifted a basket, and a large hand covered hers, warming her down to her toes.

"I'll carry that," he said, his gaze holding hers. "Pip, grab the rods."

She let go her hand and he reached for the other basket.

"No, Miss Fenwick. I'll carry that one up to the manor as well. And then you can show me the livery you'll have me wearing."

"Papa thought to give you some of his fresh linens, and I can brush out your coats. I've not found any livery at Fenwick Manor. Or...perhaps there is something stowed away in the attic. Pip, did Edie ever say whether Sir Richard's servants wore livery?"

The boy shuddered. "No."

"Did you ever meet Sir Richard," he asked the boy.

Pip's lips formed a thin line. "Aye."

She glanced at Freddy.

"Tell us about him then," she said.

Pip's face scrunched tightly. She reached for him, then pulled back her hand, sensing the boy's pride.

"He took me." He shuddered again. "Me and Lady Perry. Snatched us up on the road, one night. I was carryin' a message for Scruggs when the Squire..."

The poor boy's face clouded and he swallowed hard.

"Scruggs is the local innkeeper, Mr. Smith," she said, giving Pip time to quell his emotions. "He's been by to pay his respects to my father. Who is Lady Perry?"

"Lady Perry is Shaldon's daughter," Freddy said.

He kept his gaze on the road, not meeting her eyes.

Everyone but her knew more about these parts and the players.

She needed to educate herself, if not with Papa or Freddy, then with Edie or her new cook. It wouldn't be gossip, not truly. She needed to know just how vile Sir Richard had been.

"But you are here, Pip, whole and healthy," she said. "He let you go."

Pip's scowl deepened. "No. He told his man to shoot us. We had to jump for it. Off a cliff, into the sea." He shuddered.

Her breath caught. Sir Richard had wanted to kill a boy and a lady? "You jumped?"

She glanced at Freddy, and he gave his head a little shake.

"That's quite an adventure," Freddy said. "I'm glad to see you whole and hale."

Freddy wanted her to cease her questioning. Perhaps he was right, but...

"I had no idea just how truly bad Sir Richard was," Tilly said. "And he was involved in the smuggling hereabouts as well, I hear."

The boy's mouth clamped shut, but he finally grunted an, "Aye, miss."

"He was the real John Black, my father said."

Pip nodded. Freddy snorted, and she glanced at him. His face had taken on a grim look, quite out of character with his usual aplomb.

There was more here she didn't know, and as much as she hated gossip, she hated not knowing important things, things that everyone else seemed to know.

She must do what she usually despised—chatter on instead of asking direct questions and see if she could stir up answers.

"I'm told that there's a man sitting in the antipodes—if he survived the journey there—sentenced to transportation in place of the real John Black." They'd reached the side gate to the stable yard, and Tilly unfastened the latch. "How sad that they sentenced the wrong man."

"He was paid off," the boy said.

That supposition she *had* heard. "It's very sad, isn't it? I suppose his family needed the money."

Freddy juggled the baskets. "Off with you boy and stow those rods where you found them."

His voice crackled, and his face had gone rigid, his lips thinning.

Pip ran off with the dog at his heels, and she faced Freddy, blocking the path. "What is wrong? Why are you suddenly angry?"

His eyes burned into her, dark and glowing now. Should she encounter him on a lonely path looking like this, she *might* be afraid.

"'Tis naught," he said. "If you'll let me pass, I'll carry these in for you, miss, and you can explain to me more about my duties tonight."

She yanked a basket from his hand. "Do *not* do this. Talking about Sir Richard and John Black has made you angry. I'll know why."

He gazed at her a long moment. "Maybe that man transported wasn't paid off. Maybe he was caught in a web by corrupt officials."

Corrupt officials?

Sir Richard, of course, who'd been the Justice of the Peace. But who else had been in these parts then? The Earl of Shaldon or Lord Farnsworth?

Or...the Riding Officer. The man whose presence sent shivers down her spine, and not in a good way.

Freddy's words echoed back to her: *Greggson is corrupt.*

"*Now* may I pass, miss?"

Dark eyes studied her, anger churning in them. Not directed at her, not really.

Freddy hadn't known Pip. He was new to the area, just like herself, and yet well enough acquainted with John Black to have his own theory about the miscarriage of justice. And to be angry about it.

"You must speak to my father, Mr. Smith. You must tell him what you know. He is the Justice of the Peace here now, and there is no corruption in him."

His eyes burned into her, and he blinked, shuttering the anger, lifting the corner of his lip in the start of a cocky grin. "Only repeating what I hear, miss."

He brushed past her, his broad chest grazing her and sparking an answering heat, and then he stomped off in a direct path to the kitchens.

As if he already knew the way.

Freddy Smith. Freddy Sandford. Could he be one and the same? And why was he here?

It was a sure thing he wouldn't readily tell her. And she wouldn't have time to interrogate him until after they'd got through this blasted dinner.

"We must set one more place for tonight."

At the sound of Tilly's voice, Freddy looked up from arranging the cutlery. She cradled a silver epergne, and set it down gently, almost lovingly.

The moment she spotted him, her eyes widened, her gaze sweeping over him, color rising in her cheeks.

If a fresh shave and a clean shirt could bring that about, he'd give anything to make an appearance before her in his regimentals. He tamped down the urge to return her bold gaze, ducking his head. "Very well, miss."

When she scowled, he bit back a smile. She disliked him acting submissively.

Edie's broom stilled. "Who else is coming?"

It was no wonder this girl, Edie, had left Sir Richard's service. Keeping her place was not in her nature. He had a feeling, though, that Tilly would value her forthright ways.

Tilly set out stemware. "Mr. Greggson."

His hand slipped, and a fork clattered to the floor.

"The Riding Officer?" Edie's disgust was clear.

Tilly grimaced and nodded.

He should cry off this moment from this *service* to Sir Newton.

But dammit, he'd never been one to run. The man didn't know his face or his true name, and surely, he wouldn't bring his pistol and his cutlass to Sir Newton's dining table. Greggson was a villain, but Freddy hadn't needed Tilly's endorsement to believe in her father's honor. He had a feeling Sir Newton wouldn't clamp him in irons and ship him off to join his brother.

Lord Farnsworth, he wasn't sure about.

Tilly sighed. "Greggson was visiting Lord Farnsworth when Papa...when my father called. Father didn't think he could very well exclude the man."

"Besides which..." Edie paused, bit her lip, and shook her head.

"Besides which what, Edie?" Tilly asked.

Edie slid her gaze to him, assessing.

This bit of news he needed to hear. "I'm the soul of discretion," he said. "I don't gossip."

"It's not gossip," Edie said. "Well it might be, but it's gossip you should know about, miss. Though it's said he carries on with the inn maid, the Riding Officer is putting it about that he's...he's *courting* you."

"*What?*" A glass crashed.

Edie blanched too much for one as bold as her. She had hesitated over her choice of words, which meant, Greggson's talk in the village had been about something coarser than courting.

Oh, aye, Greggson would want to force a marriage with Tilly for a chance at the manor holding and the suspicion of hidden money, but it would be no desire for the lovely woman that drove him, not with his wench stashed away at the inn.

"Oh blast it, we have so little crystal to spare," Tilly muttered. "Yet I fear I shall be hard pressed not to break a plate over his head as well."

He went to help her with the shards of broken glass. "Do not worry," he said. "I'll be here to intervene. I'll wrest the plate from your hands and use my fists on him."

Their gazes met, and color rose again in her cheeks, and likely his, since heat surged in him.

That wouldn't do.

"Are you all right, miss?"

She huffed out a breath and nodded. "Thank you. And though we can ill afford to lose dishes, Mr. Smith, I don't want you in a tangle with the Riding Officer." She dusted her hands. "What shall we call you tonight? Frederick? Or Smith? Father and I have never employed a footman."

At his home and his friends' homes, footmen were always called by their first name. But Greggson might have stumbled across the full name of the transported man's brother.

"In some great houses, all the coachmen are called John, and all the footmen James, or so I've heard," he said, improvising.

"James, then, for tonight. I'll tell Father."

"And where are you from, *James*?" Edie asked. "Some great folk are nosy, so best come prepared for that sort of prying as well."

"From York," Tilly said. "When the other locals left, I urged Papa to write to a friend there for help."

Edie blinked. "Is it true? You're bringing people from York to take good work?"

"It seems I must. Sir Richard's ghost is forcing my hand. Though it's not my first choice. I'd much rather share what wealth there is employing the local people."

"Hmm," Edie said, and went back to her sweeping.

He caught Tilly's eye and winked. "Some folk might decide they'd rather brave a ghost than lose good jobs to fresh folk."

"Then they have only to call at the manor and speak to me."

"Sir Newton ought to hire a steward to deal with those sorts of calls," Edie said. "That's the usual way, I hear, at the grand houses."

He was a fool for opening this can of worms. The last thing he needed was a steward and housemaids underfoot.

Tilly laughed ruefully. "I suppose you are right. Fenwick Manor was grand two hundred years ago, but it isn't now, is it?"

"Not yet," he said. But he had a feeling with Tilly at the helm it would be soon, with or without a hidden treasure.

Tilly set out the precious candles in the hall while Freddy—she must remember to call him James tonight—worked at lighting the temperamental lamp.

"You look lovely tonight, miss," he said.

Surely her cheeks had flushed, making her thankful for the dim lighting. Heavens, she'd all but drooled on the man earlier. With a clean shave, fresh linens, and his coats well-brushed, Freddy looked deliciously firm-jawed and handsome himself.

And she must not go down that path.

"Though I've never employed a footman before, I believe that would be a cheeky thing for one to say to his employer, *James*."

The floorboard squeaked and Papa appeared, wearing his finest attire. "Cheeky, but true," he said, dropping a kiss on her forehead. "You are altogether beautiful. More precious than rubies."

"Song of Songs and Proverbs. You are mixing your Bible verses again, Papa."

"And her ways are pleasant ways," Freddy—James said. He smiled, and she had to turn away.

"You are familiar with scripture, er, James?" Papa asked.

"My mother had a yen for Proverbs."

Freddy had come from a God-fearing home.

"So much wisdom there," Papa said, chattering on.

The guests would arrive soon, and her insides were quaking. Hosting a dinner at the vicar's humble home differed greatly from serving as hostess for a baronet with a lord in attendance.

She'd dressed her hair carefully and donned her best gown, a lavender she'd had made by the village seamstress for her mother's half-mourning. For Cumberland society, it had been more than sufficient for the vicar's plain spinster daughter. When they'd attended dinners with the local gentry, the daughters and wives attired in dresses made up from the latest fashion plates, she'd seen with her own eyes where her gown lacked. Oh, how she wished to have something finer, and a man like Freddy nearby to notice.

She shook herself. It didn't matter. She'd never have a season in Edinburgh or York, much less London, so there was no sense fashing, as her mother would have said, about gowns she would never have.

The door knocker rattled, and she straightened, smoothing her skirts.

Freddy...James had slipped away to see to the dining room. Papa opened the door and welcomed their guests.

Both men bowed over her hand. Lord Farnsworth was a man of middle years—in fact he was altogether middling, in height and appearance, but perfectly mannered.

Greggson, on the other hand, lingered over her fingers, his eyes sweeping her from head to foot.

Perhaps that worked with his tavern maid. *She* wanted to slap him.

She picked up the candelabra. "Since we are all here, shall we go up to dinner?"

"Lead the way, my dear," Papa said.

Greggson took the candles from her. "I'll take this, and you may take my arm."

Lord Farnsworth stepped up, offering his arm. "Allow me the honor, Miss Fenwick." He smiled. "Rank has some privileges, Greggson."

Here was a man who had seen her discomfort. Had she been so obvious?

Greggson's laugh was false. There was no true friendship between these two men.

It was going to be a very long dinner.

CHAPTER NINE

With two brothers and a series of tutors with sturdy canes, Freddy *had* learned the skill of keeping a straight face. Exercising that skill tonight was requiring extreme effort.

Farnsworth seemed decent enough, the sort of chap who, when required to carry out his duties for King and country, would readily slice a man's throat. Not the sort to molest an affable ex-vicar and his daughter, though.

Greggson was another matter. He'd observed the Riding Officer from a distance. Up close, the man's gentility smelled of musty linens and that persistent stench of corruption.

It was all he could do to hold back from sloshing soup on the devil's intricately tied neck cloth.

"And how do you find life at the Manor, Miss Fenwick?" Farnsworth asked.

Tilly hesitated, picking her words. "The manor is...fascinating. And quite a bit larger than the vicarage in Cumberland."

"And harder to staff," Greggson said. "Miss Fenwick has had trouble keeping servants. Where did you find this fellow?"

She blinked. "I did tell you that we were making arrangements with Father's acquaintances in York, did I not?"

Freddy swallowed a smile. The vicar's daughter had handily avoided an outright lie.

Greggson smirked. "What about you, Sir Newton? Have you also found Fenwick Manor *fascinating*?"

The squire glanced at the man and tipped a spoonful of mock turtle soup, closing his eyes and lingering over the flavor. "Excellent soup, my dear. You've done well."

Tilly sent her father a smile that managed to be both proud and demure.

"Yes, well," Sir Newton said. "The library here is quite the thing for a man such as myself. Books, books, and more books, stacked everywhere, eh Matilda? Matilda has been assessing their arrangement while I work away on my manuscript."

"And rebuilding your stone walls?" Greggson raised an eyebrow.

"Yes, yes. Matilda has a mind to raise Blackface sheep. Lord Shaldon is sending some down from his estate in the north. She would like to confine them when they arrive until we determine the best grazing."

While Freddy cleared away soup bowls, Farnsworth commenced a discussion of sheep and wool prices that led to talk of weavers and whether the troubles would spill into their area. Eventually they came around to the topic of the free trade.

"Have you found all of Sir Richard's hiding places?" Greggson asked.

Freddy steadied his hand on the serving dish.

This. This was why he was here so exposed. He cared naught about sheep or weavers. He needed to spy on *this* conversation.

"If we said yes, how could we possibly be sure we'd found them all?" Tilly asked. "Though I confess a great curiosity about Sir Richard and his smuggling. How on earth could he carry on so long and right under the nose of the local authorities?"

Edie's arrival with the fish course interrupted the possibility of an admission of guilt by the Riding Officer. Edie deposited her platter and left.

"*That* was a local woman, wasn't she?" Greggson asked. "Not from York, I think. I recall seeing her about the village."

"You are very interested in the servants, Greggson," Farnsworth observed.

"I'm only looking to be of assistance to the new Squire and Miss Fenwick." He smiled at Tilly.

"Yes. Mr. Greggson even had a housekeeper in mind for us, my lord," Tilly said.

Farnsworth bestowed a half smile on her. "Did he indeed? Are you not still lodging at Scruggs's inn, Greggson?"

"I am," Greggson said.

Oh, aye, it was said smoothly enough. And no doubt the housekeeper he'd proposed for them was the barmaid he was swiving.

"But I hear things here and about and I'm always willing to help my neighbors."

She glanced up at Freddy as he served her. "I'm quite pleased with the staff I've recently hired."

Her look had been arch, not at all flirtatious, but he struggled to quell a grin.

Greggson pressed his lips tight on a grimace and managed a fake smile, turning his oily charm on the squire. "As to your daughter's previous question about Sir Richard's hiding places, Sir Newton," he said, "perhaps there is a map of all of his buildings and hideaways, or an architectural record of the house in the library or muniments room."

Farnsworth raised an eyebrow. "Are you inquiring as part of your smuggling duties?"

"There is a rumor, which you've probably heard, that there is a treasure still hidden in this house."

"Treasure?" Tilly exclaimed. "So that was no ordinary ransacking of the manor before we arrived. What sort of treasure is here? Gold? Jewels?"

Greggson opened his mouth, closed it. "Probably both. All the more reason to be careful of who you hire. And yes, my lord, I have a duty to combat local smuggling and bring offenders to justice."

"A treasure," Tilly said again, setting down her fork.

"Pah." Sir Newton stabbed at his fish. "Likely the housebreakers found it already. The only treasure here is the library. A fine collection of books, it is. So glad the housebreakers did not take the books with the gold and the jewels."

"The library *is* lovely," Tilly said. "Though tidying it and cataloguing the work is a task I've still to tackle. And as for treasures—I've seen none in the nooks and crannies I've investigated." Her fork hung in the air over her plate. "Speaking of the free trade, Mr. Greggson, were you involved in the capture of the false John Black?"

Greggson swallowed, coughed, and took a hurried sip of his wine.

"What a sad affair that was," Sir Newton said. "Such a tragic miscarriage of justice."

"The man accepted a bribe to take that punishment," Greggson choked out. "I have no sympathy for him."

"Truly?" Tilly asked. "Not a glimmer of pity for the man and his family?" She pinned the Riding Officer with a sharp look. "But you have not answered my question, Mr. Greggson. Were you involved in his capture?"

"Not directly. I was in the Whitby area then."

Farnsworth's fingers drummed the table, making no noise. "As I recall, you testified at his trial."

"That is true. I had moved to this area around the time of his capture. I was proud to be able to add my testimony."

"Proud to add testimony against an innocent man?" Tilly asked.

The room went silent, tension quaking across the table. Sir Newton and Farnsworth observed while Freddy held his breath, ready to dash the Riding Officer with the platter of fish sauce.

Greggson scoffed. "Miss Fenwick, innocent men do not take money to suffer another man's punishment."

Tilly's back stiffened, as well it should. Greggson was a fool if he thought to bully her at her father's table.

"And yet," she said, her voice cracking, "do you not feel a certain sense of shame that because the authorities did not capture the right man, a great villain like our late cousin could continue his ways?"

Tilly, Tilly. She was magnificent. Unyielding. She would make a great field commander.

"Perhaps a little more effort on the part of the officers of the Crown," Tilly said, "and the substitution would have been found and the true culprit brought to justice. Indeed, Lord Farnsworth, do you not think the Home Office should investigate how such a miscarriage of justice could happen in England?"

Greggson broke the long silence with a laugh and his fork clattered onto his plate.

"Such a passion for justice your daughter has, Sir Newton. An admirable quality in a lady. But, Miss Fenwick, if we track down the family of that man who was transported in place of Sir Richard, we'll find them living in luxury from the money Sir Richard paid them, and the Crown will have to bring charges against them for the fraud."

Farnsworth exchanged a look with Sir Newton, and then his hooded gaze landed on Freddy.

Freddy hastened his way. "More, my lord?"

Farnsworth shook his head.

"How much money did the family receive?" Tilly asked.

"We don't know that," Greggson said.

"Did you not interrogate Sir Richard when he was captured, Mr. Greggson?"

"Mr. Greggson was not involved in the capture or interrogation of Sir Richard," Farnsworth said. "I am not at liberty to give details, but we did ascertain then that the man transported as John Black was a substitute for Sir Richard."

"And thus a criminal in his own right," Greggson said. "Paid off the by the old squire."

"Is that certain?" Tilly asked. "Did the family in fact receive the money?" She waved a hand. "Oh, I understand you may not disclose details, Lord Farnsworth. I am not pressing you for them, not truly, only speculating." Her shoulders rose with an indignant breath. "So many poor people are starving now. What justice is there in calling a man a criminal for trying to feed his family? And what if...what if Sir Richard didn't pay the money? He was enough of a villain to have cheated the man."

Greggson laughed again. "Good heavens, Miss Fenwick. How you go on."

"Matilda makes a fair point," Sir Newton said.

She nodded to her father and glanced at Lord Farnsworth. "And, think of this, gentlemen. Worse than our supposition about a bribe—Sir Richard was the Justice of the Peace hereabouts, was he not? What if the man's capture was the result of corruption among the authorities?"

The tray crashed on the buffet, juice sloshing, and he hastened to mop the spill, glancing back at Boudica.

She was letting out a breath and looking around the table. Greggson's cheeks had gone red, his thin lips rimmed in white. Farnsworth and Sir Newton were eyeing the Riding Officer.

"Oh, do forgive me," Tilly said. "I am shocking all of you. You will say this is the musing of a fanciful woman, won't you, Mr. Greggson? I must hasten to tell you that Father and I have seen appalling hunger in England. If Papa and I find that treasure you mentioned, I shall beg him to put it to good use, not just in improvements to the manor. No one in this district shall suffer hunger as long as my father is Squire here, isn't that right, Papa?"

She and her father exchanged fond smiles.

"Now," she said, "What think you of this fish, Lord Farnsworth? It is fresh from our stream."

When she turned her gaze to Farnsworth, Greggson cast her a venomous look, then blinked it away and answered a question from Sir Newton.

Freddy's insides roiled with the need to plant his fist in the Riding Officer's face.

A brave woman, was his Tilly. She'd been fishing all right today—in the morning for their meal, in the afternoon when she questioned him, and tonight for the information she somehow knew he wanted.

She was a brave woman, and an intuitive one, and one who had just provoked a weaselly enemy.

As he carried around the next course, he met Farnsworth's gaze.

Whether Farnsworth was a friend was uncertain, but it seemed his lordship was the enemy of Freddy's enemy, and for now, that was enough.

"I shall leave you men to your brandy," Tilly said, standing.

Freddy began clearing dishes and Edie popped in from the kitchen to carry away serving dishes.

"Perhaps we should all join you," Greggson said. "I should love to see this library you spoke of, Sir Newton."

He set down the stack of china, prepared to follow the man out.

"I need you in the kitchen," Edie whispered at his elbow.

He nodded.

"I should like to restore order in the library before I conduct any tours," Tilly said. "Enjoy your brandy."

Sir Newton glanced at Farnsworth, and then he caught Freddy's eye.

"I'll allow it," Sir Newton said. "Matilda, escort Mr. Greggson to the library. I'd ask that you not disturb the papers on my desk, please, and...er...James here will light your way. James, take the extra candles, and keep the stacks from falling on our guest. Edie, fetch us a fresh bottle of brandy if you please."

It was clear enough to him, and it must be to Greggson also—his job was to keep the Riding Officer from falling on Tilly.

A plate clattered behind him.

He went to the sideboard and helped Edie gather the fallen cutlery. "I'll be down later."

"You'd better," she whispered.

He grabbed a brace of candles and hastened out after the Riding Officer.

He'd protect Tilly, and he'd get a fresh look at that library.

CHAPTER TEN

Tilly ignored the arm offered her and insisted on holding a candle instead.

Both men followed her, Freddy trailing behind with more light, as was his due, being a servant and her protector.

"Careful of the wax, James," she called over her shoulder. "These runners are old but we must make them last a bit longer."

"Yes, miss," he boomed out.

The deep voice soothed her. He was reminding her—and Greggson—he was present.

Freddy outweighed Greggson by at least two stones, and she had a feeling that in his true identity he also outranked the slimy toad of a Riding Officer.

She must find a way to discover both men's secrets.

For now, though, her mission was getting Greggson in and out of the library without the man laying a hand on Papa's things or on her. Why had Papa allowed him this private tour?

She stumbled, her breath catching. Papa had sent all four of them away—herself, Greggson,

Freddy and Edie. He was having a private conversation with Farnsworth.

Greggson had been at Gorse Point Cottage when Papa visited there and the unctuous man had wheedled an invitation to dinner and then he'd timed his arrival to coincide with Lord Farnsworth's. Papa hadn't had a moment alone with Lord Farnsworth.

And whatever Greggson wanted to see in the library was more important to him than preventing a private conversation between the two older men.

It made her head spin. She must spend more time in this library finding its secrets.

"For heaven's sake, let me hold the light," Greggson said.

She straightened the taper. "No, no, thank you."

Greggson had been angry at dinner, angry about her questioning. If anyone was involved with a corrupt arrest, it would be Mr. Greggson.

When the opportunity arose, she must pressure him more.

When they reached the library, she pushed open the door, the hinges squealing in protest. At once, the chill, the remains of Papa's earlier fire, and the smell of old leather filled her.

A sharp wind snuffed out her candle.

Papa had forgot to close the windows.

"I'll get that." Freddy set the brace of candles on the edge of the desk.

While he closed the windows, Tilly pushed aside the ladder-back chair Papa kept for visitors, relit her candle from one of the flickering tapers and led Greggson to the center of the room.

"Has the rain started yet?" she asked.

"No, miss."

Greggson's gaze traveled the room.

What was he looking for?

"I believe it will be quite a storm," she said. "Mr. Greggson, we should make this a short tour, else you'll have a very wet ride back to your lodging. What in particular would you like to see?"

"Sir Newton is correct. He has quite a collection here. Can you tell me how these books are arranged?"

"How they are arranged?" She flung out a hand toward the towering stacks of books that lay, spines out, one atop another obscuring the shelving behind. "In total disarray, as you see."

Freddy stepped up behind her, bringing the comforting scent of Papa's shaving soap that he'd borrowed.

She took in a deep breath. She must move this along.

She pointed to the corner of the room near her father's desk. "I can tell you that over there are classics, books in Latin and Greek, lovely old books with leather bindings that have not mildewed. I've gone through several and the print is unsmudged and readable."

Greggson scoffed. "You also read Latin and Greek?" He took a step toward the corner and paused at the desk where books weighted the loose papers of Papa's manuscripts.

"I do. And I must say that my father is most particular that his papers not be disturbed. He allows no one to touch them."

Greggson angled his head over the desk, reading.

"What is this?" he asked. "*Freddy's story of a hobgoblin*?" He bent down further.

Freddy moved quickly and removed the brace of candles he'd left on the desk and carried away the light. "I'm sorry, miss, I forgot about the papers. I'm afraid I've dripped a bit of wax."

"Oh, dear."

"I'll come back and clean it," Freddy said.

With the light removed, Greggson slipped into deep shadows and she couldn't see his reaction.

"Yes, thank you," she said.

"I thought Sir Newton allowed no one in to touch his papers," Greggson said.

"We shall see what he says, now that we have a manservant."

Had Papa had enough time with Lord Farnsworth?

She picked up the candle she'd brought. "Come, we'll circle the room. Bring the light, James. Over here, I believe are mostly novels and poetry. I've wondered if Sir Richard or one of our other ancestors was a great reader."

Greggson dragged a finger over the top book in a stack that reached as high as his chest and looked at it, grimacing.

"Pardon the dust. I've knocked most of the cobwebs away, but I've not had time or staff for a thorough cleaning." Removing, dusting, cataloguing, and arranging the shelved books would be a daunting task, one she'd relish if she had time and servants.

"The fireplace wall, as you'll see, has only a meager collection on the nearby shelves. These appear to be mostly sermons and other edifying texts. And over here," they crossed the room, "is a wall filled with periodicals, agricultural guides, and newspapers."

"I imagine the mice are enjoying those," Greggson said.

Having imagined the same thing, she'd been feeding the unbound newspapers surreptitiously into the fire.

Greggson pivoted, surveying the dark corners of the room. "And somewhere in here will be an architectural rendering of the house and the holdings with all the old squire's hiding places."

She shrugged. "Misfiled, perhaps."

"With Sir Richard's ledgers, perhaps?"

They hadn't yet found Sir Richard's ledgers, or if Papa had received them from the solicitor in York, he hadn't mentioned it.

"I wouldn't know."

"Or perhaps in your father's desk?"

A burst of wind rattled the windows and blew down the chimney.

"I wouldn't presume to go through my father's desk. Now, we should rejoin him and Lord Farnsworth. The weather is turning."

"I suppose I should be on my way. You, man, run to the stable and tell them to bring my horse around."

Freddy shifted the candles, fisting his hand.

"Nonsense." Tilly bit back a harsher retort. "We'll send the kitchen boy." She went to the door, holding it open until Greggson stepped through. Freddy's light followed them down the corridor to the dining room.

She handed Greggson her candle. "Please join the others while I have a word with my footman."

Greggson eyed her speculatively and slipped into the dining room, the heavy door closing on him.

A chill draft wafted through the corridor and she shivered. She gripped Freddy's arm and led him further away. "Will you hurry and send word for the horses? The weather is turning foul. I should not like to have to offer that man shelter."

"And while I'm running this errand, where will you be?"

"I'll join them and let Lord Farnsworth know it is high time to leave if he wishes to outpace the storm." Another shiver went through her. "More politely stated of course."

His lips quirked. "Of course. Let me escort you back in."

She shook her head. "Take the servants' pass-through. It will be quicker and no one will try to send you off on another errand."

He handed her the brace of candles.

"You'll need them to navigate that passage," she said.

"Very well, miss. If you need me, you have only to call. That wall is thin."

Heat rose in her cheeks, and she was glad to step back into shadows. "Off with you, then."

She watched his light move down the corridor and then turned and stepped into the dining room.

The lone lit candle sat off on the distant sideboard and the rest of the room was dark.

An arm snaked around her shoulder.

"Miss Fenwick, how well you have arranged this."

An unpleasant male musk filled her senses, and all of her muscles tightened.

Papa was not here, nor Lord Farnsworth. But...*please God*...rescue was not so far away.

"Do remove your hand, Mr. Greggson." She shouted the words at the doorway that led to the servant's passage.

"I think not."

He whipped her around and bent his head toward her. She dodged away, and his hands framed her head, turning her to him.

"Stop this now," she shouted, arching away from his fishy breath.

Her backside hit the table. She brought her knee up sharply and Greggson flew away, crashing into the wall.

She clutched a chair back, struggling for breath. What had just happened? And why? And how...a tall figure advanced on her. Her pulse spiked, and then eased. She couldn't make out a face, but the scent was her Papa's soap.

It was Freddy. Trembling, she flung herself at him and fell into a tight embrace.

"Are you all right?"

Nearby, Greggson moaned, and in the corridor footsteps clattered. Freddy was wise to whisper. Greggson wasn't unconscious.

She snuggled against his shoulder, relishing a warmth no man had ever offered her. Freddy had rescued her. He'd risked much—Greggson was a dangerous man.

Murmurs in the corridor grew closer, and Greggson groaned more loudly. She untangled herself and stepped back. "Go. Papa's coming, and Greggson is coming to."

Greggson stirred, and Freddy stepped toward him.

She grabbed his arm and tugged him along toward the servant's door.

"Go," she whispered.

"No. Your father—"

"Will protect me. Us."

His dark gaze melted her, heat uncoiling deep within her. Freddy had honor, and courage, and strength. He'd saved her, and now she must save him.

"Us?" The word whispered through her, their lips almost touching. "Tilly—"

Cloth rustled as Greggson stirred.

"No." She shook her head. "Here." She handed Freddy the single taper she'd been carrying. His own brace of candles rested on the sideboard near the servant's passage. He was lucky Greggson hadn't spotted him.

Gloved fingers cradled her cheek, spiking more warmth.

"I'll be right here, on the other side."

She nodded and pulled the door closed on Freddy's boot. Papa's footsteps moved closer, but Greggson's arms and legs were moving as well.

One serving tray remained, laden with cutlery. She grabbed a sharp knife just as the corridor door opened, admitting her father and Lord Farnsworth.

Papa froze, the lamp he held lighting his features, his gaze landing upon the knife in her hand. "Tilly?"

She let out a long breath and followed his line of sight to her trembling hand.

Freddy peered through the slit in the door opening, anger still quaking inside him. How dare Greggson touch the lass?

It wouldn't happen again. He'd see to it, just as soon as he had a moment alone with the mawworm.

"Tilly," Sir Newton said again, and there was astonishment in the older man's voice. "Whatever has happened, my dear?"

The voice grew louder as the Squire approached.

"What is going on here, Greggson?" Sir Newton asked sharply.

"Mr. Greggson surely stumbled," Tilly said. "In the dark. We didn't know you'd left and when we returned, you'd put out all the lights on the table except those."

"That's quite a stumble." Farnsworth must have drawn nearer, as his voice carried more clearly. "I'll fetch you a brandy, Greggson, though perhaps you had more than enough wine to have hit the wall so handily."

"Thank you," Greggson said. "Actually, I fear I must have a private word with you, Sir Newton."

"A private word? Tilly, where is the footman?"

Freddy held his breath, waiting for her reply.

"I sent him to alert the stables. Mr. Greggson wanted to leave before the rain worsens and I thought perhaps you would wish to return safely home also, Lord Farnsworth."

His heart lifted. She was not just lovely, but smart to boot and she could work her away around the truth without telling an outright lie.

"I fear I must talk to you tonight, sir," Greggson said, clearing his throat.

The hair on Freddy's neck rose as his fists clenched.

"You see," Greggson said, "Miss Fenwick and I—"

"Saw the ghost," Tilly blurted out. She reached for her father's hand tugging him towards her.

"The ghost, my dear?"

"Yes, Papa. I hesitated to say it. It was the most astonishing thing."

Oh, she was breathless, gathering her thoughts, and he wanted to cheer. Fair of face and fast on her feet was his Tilly.

"One minute, Mr. Greggson and I were wondering where you and Lord Farnsworth had got to, and the next Mr. Greggson was thrown against the wall."

He swallowed a chuckle. All true enough.

"By the ghost?" Farnsworth asked. "Did you see it, Greggson?"

"No, and—"

"But of course you didn't, Mr. Greggson. You were looking at me and the ghost came up behind you. It was...spectral...my lord. It was...light and shadow. Oh, I don't know how to express this."

A hand tweaked Freddy's elbow. Edie had come up from the kitchen.

He put a finger to his lips and led her aside. "Leave the dishes and go along home," he hissed. "I promise I'll set them to soak. And on your way out, tell the stable boy to bring the guests' horses around."

Edie raised an eyebrow. "The ghost threw the Riding Officer against the wall?"

He gripped both of her shoulders. "It's as you said, Edie. He's after her. Don't spread this about until I deal with things."

"Is that what the footmen in York do?"

"Just go." He turned her toward the staircase.

"You'll tell me everything," she whispered.

Not likely. He pushed open the dining-room door and marched through.

Greggson was tipping back a brandy. Tilly stood next to her father, still gripping her knife.

"Did you see aught in the passageway or the stairs?" she asked.

He blinked. "No, miss. I've only just returned from sending that message you asked for. And now I've come for that last tray."

"You saw no one?" Greggson asked.

"I saw the maid on the stairs," he said. "I told her I'd carry down whatever dishes were left. Is something amiss?"

Tilly pressed her hand to her chest. "I don't believe in ghosts," she said, her voice shaking. "At least I didn't. Papa, we must go back to your library and write this down while my memory of the details is still fresh. Gentlemen, we will see you out."

Greggson's glass crashed to the table. "I would come along and speak to you first, Sir Newton."

"It will wait," Papa said firmly. "The rain shall be pelting anyone who's about in it soon. You may call on me tomorrow, Greggson."

Freddy watched until they'd all departed, then he carried the tray down to the deserted kitchen and slipped out.

He tucked his head down and slipped around to the front of the house where the two men were mounting their horses. On a night like this, Greggson wouldn't ride like Sir Richard's ghost was chasing him. Anyone following would be able to keep up afoot.

After Tilly's rejection, Greggson would head for the tavern wench's bed. Hell, even if he'd walked out of the manor with his nuptials arranged, he'd have returned to the barmaid. Tonight, though, he'd be in no mood for swiving, not after Freddy had finished with him.

CHAPTER ELEVEN

While he sheltered in the shadows of the innyard, Freddy watched the lightning flashing in the western sky and counted out the seconds for the crackle of thunder. Still a good many miles distant, but likely to move closer.

Greggson had taken his time, picking his way on the slippery road after Farnsworth rode off at the crossroads. Now the Riding Officer was dismounting and bellowing for the ostler.

He'd finish this business then get back to his hiding place.

An old man trudged out and took the horse's lead, waving away Greggson's curses. Before Freddy could step out, a hand gripped his elbow.

He pulled his arm back for a punch.

"It's Farnsworth."

Farnsworth. He gazed down at the shorter man. How the devil had he arrived here before Greggson? And where was his mount?

"Well met, Mr. Smith," he said.

Freddy blinked, buying time. "What are you doing here, my lord?"

"There's trouble afoot tonight. Word of a boat coming in."

"A boat?" A smuggling load. His chest tightened. If they thought to implicate him... His mother couldn't lose another son to false charges. "That has *naught* to do with me."

"No? You're not hovering about the inn to volunteer your services?"

Anger simmered in him. "My business is with the Riding Officer."

"Yes, the lovely Mr. Greggson. Sir Newton did tell me you were only hired temporarily and that clever bit about you coming from York was a tale told for Greggson's sake, I assume."

He glanced back at the innyard. Greggson had disappeared.

Chasing him into the taproom, out in the open, with all the locals about, would be foolish. He'd have to catch him later tonight—if the man planned to go after the smugglers. More likely he'd taken his bribe and was heading to bed, and Freddy would have to bide his time until another dark night.

"I'll just take my leave," Freddy said. He could come back around and see whether the Riding Officer appeared again.

"He's a bad sort," Farnsworth said. "Vindictive. I wonder, does he believe in ghosts, like the one who tossed him about tonight?"

The simmering anger subsided. There was no sense dissembling more. Farnsworth was no fool, and he might be a help to Tilly. "He sought to compromise Til—Miss Fenwick."

"Be assured, her father won't entertain an offer from him, no matter what happened."

"Nothing—"

"Yes. I know, a ghost intervened before Greggson could assault her. Best get to your bed before the crews go out and this storm worsens.

I'll be at Gorse Point Cottage for some weeks. When you have what you're looking for come and talk to me."

He watched Farnsworth slip off into the night, as quietly as he'd appeared. Another burst of lightning showed he had vanished. The electrical charge in the air sent ripples through him.

When I have what I'm looking for?

Farnsworth knew.

When the door closed on their guests, Tilly turned on her father.

"I must tell you the truth, Papa," she said.

He picked up the candles and took her hand in his. "You're cold. Come, we'll go to the library. You have a shawl there I think, and you may have a glass of sherry."

Her hands might be cold but anger swelled in her, closing her throat. She'd never been in this spot with a man before. No man had ever dared such effrontery. She choked in a breath. "I must confess, Papa. There's no ghost story to write."

"Then we can just sit and talk, the way we used to do in our little vicarage in Cumberland." He squeezed her hand as he led her along. "What an excellent dinner you arranged for us. I'm quite happier with this cook than with the last. Do you think she will stay?"

He chattered on about the soup, the fish, the roast and the sauces, calming the rage in her, and when they reached the library, he seated her, stirred the embers, and brought her a drink.

"I must apologize," Papa said. "Lord Farnsworth needed to step away for a...er...privy break, and I supposed we would find you in the library after. But when we arrived there you were gone. What did Mr. Greggson do?"

Blood surged in her, making her heart pound. "He pushed me up against the dining table. I believe he was trying to kiss me. Or worse." A shudder went through her. "I...I tried to give him a sharp kick as Mama once taught me."

"And he crashed all the way into the wall?"

She shook her head and swallowed. "Freddy came up behind and pulled him off me. It was dark, and I don't believe Mr. Greggson saw him. I made up the ghost bit to protect Freddy."

"That was quick thinking. I suppose you are risking our cook and our new housekeeper though with this talk of a ghost."

She thought about the sharp-eyed housekeeper. Edie didn't miss much, and neither she nor Rose appeared to be flighty. "I think not. They both worked here when Sir Richard was squire. He was far more fearsome than any ghost, even his own." She took a breath. "Plus, Papa, Edie, the maid, informed me that Mr. Greggson was spreading it about the village that he is courting me."

"Was he?"

Papa's voice had cracked on those words, as though he were angry. Papa never displayed anger. She'd never seen him enraged. He'd never raised his voice to either her, her mother, or any servant.

Lightning flashed and illuminated the room and she saw the truth of it—Papa's face was set into a hard mask.

"Edie also said he is...he is *carrying on* with a maid at the inn where he resides."

Papa's lips pressed together. "Yes. I have heard that."

"Do not fret, Papa. Nothing more happened with Mr. Greggson. Should he offer for me, I will not accept, and I'll spread the ghost story about to protect Freddy."

"If he would attack you in your own home after dining at table with us, how will you go about the estate safely seeing to your new sheep and such?"

"I shall take Wulver with me. She doesn't like him."

"I fear even Wulver can be over-matched by a determined man."

He was right. Wulver would give a good fight, but a man with a cutlass and pistols on his belt could stop her.

She could never allow harm to come to the gentle dog. Nor could she bear to be confined indoors and followed about everywhere by a footman, if they had a genuine one. Freddy's presence though would be a comfort.

"I believe he was angling to shelter here tonight to ride out the storm," Papa mused.

A sliver of dread ran down her spine. It would have been the neighborly thing to offer shelter to both guests on a night like this. Greggson would have sneaked about looking for her bedchamber to complete his conquest. Or...

"What is this treasure he spoke of, Papa?"

"Hmm." Papa carried the candle to his desk, and she followed him. He looked at her speculatively and then pulled out a drawer, removing the papers stacked therein.

Then he pried up the drawer's bottom and pulled out a rolled parchment.

Her heart pounded, and she bit her tongue.

"I found this, poking around in this desk. I assumed my late cousin would have safes and secret compartments, not just hideaways for his smuggling goods." Papa lifted the thick roll.

"Here is one of the articles I believe Mr. Greggson was seeking."

He picked up his reading glasses, shuffled over to the table, lit more candles and unrolled the sheets of parchment.

"Here you see, is the plan of the house rendered sometime in the last century. I confess, daughter, I've not just been in here behind closed doors writing ghost stories. I've been pouring over this from time to time, looking for the location of the muniments room. Also, reviewing Sir Richard's ledgers." He waved to a pile of books she'd not seen before. "That stack is all I have of the old squire's records. Yet, the Fenwicks are an ancient family, and so there should be documents going back as far as the Domesday Book."

"Where did you get those, Papa?"

"The solicitor in York who was settling Sir Richard's estate had them."

"Surely he had older records as well if he established your right to the inheritance."

"He had enough to go back and trace our entitlement, but no further." Papa frowned. "And you should know there was an issue. A possible claim on the property."

"A claim?"

"Yes, and a recent one at that, during Sir Richard's lifetime, made by a descendent of a distaff branch of the Fenwick family. There'd been a question of legitimacy the claimant said he could resolve."

Her mind muddled through his words. Someone else had claimed their home? "What—"

"No, you must not worry. The claim was dropped. Fenwick Manor will be your home after I am gone." He traced a finger over the parchment stopping at a square. "Look here. This is the room we're in. And over here is the dining room and the parlour. You can see the servants' passages here and here." He outlined the passages that ran along the dining room and the parlor. "In these other areas in this old wing of the house, the rooms, including this library, are flanked by empty spaces. Wide enough for servants' pass-throughs."

He was pointing to the walls around the library.

"Edie showed me the one adjoining Sir Richard's bedchamber."

He nodded. "During the Revolution, the Fenwicks maintained their Catholic faith, secretly until deciding to change sides strategically to maintain their wealth."

"Did they truly wall up the priests when they went over to Cromwell?"

"Such stories of atrocities are gruesome, even for the Fenwicks. You must not worry about the events of two centuries ago. No, the evil that Sir Richard wrought is far more fearsome." He reached for her hand and patted it. "You questioned Greggson most severely at dinner about the man who was transported. Why?"

She took in a shaky breath. "Did I embarrass you, Papa? Was I too forward?"

"Matilda," he chided, "what do you know?"

What she *knew* had nothing to do with it—it was what she *sensed*. She shook her head. Perhaps she was more like her superstitious Papa than she realized.

"When we were fishing this morning, Edie's young cousin told us..." She took a deep breath. She wasn't sure Papa knew this story. "Sir Richard captured the boy and the Earl's daughter, and they escaped being shot—*shot*, Papa—by Sir Richard's man. They saved themselves by jumping into the sea."

She hadn't yet seen the Yorkshire coast, but from the one seaside visit she'd made as a child, she could imagine how fearful such a plunge would be. Truly, not much frightened her, but the incessant pounding of the waves had made her heart race.

"The boy told the story of Sir Richard paying off a man to be arrested in his place. Freddy...that is, Mr. Smith...seemed angry about that. When I asked him why, he said the man arrested might *not* have been paid off by Sir Richard. He might have been accused, tried, and transported by *corrupt officials*."

Papa took off his glasses and rubbed the bridge of his nose. "If it's true, what a fearsome injustice. Ripped from his family, spending month upon month chained on a ship, and at the end, delivered into a hot wilderness and put to hard labor."

"Papa," she whispered. "I believe Freddy's presence here has something to do with that injustice. I don't know what." That was her intuition again, sparking in her. Freddy's presence was a mystery, and she knew little about him except that he kept turning up and...she trusted him. "Perhaps he was in the dale that night looking for the treasure, or..." She shook her head. "Or something else. I don't know what. He's no friend to Greggson."

Another flash of lightning lit the room. This time the thunder followed more quickly, rattling the windows.

"Roll this up, please, my dear, and put it away while I cover the embers. I don't want you going about the estate on your own, Tilly. We shall explore the house and walk the grounds together when the weather is not so foul. For now, I think you'd best go to bed and lock your door."

"I should bring Wulver in."

"Let her rest in the stables tonight. I don't want you out in this weather. Now, go to bed and lock your door."

"And you'll do the same? You won't sit up all night writing?"

He touched the tip of her nose and smiled. "I won't sit up all night writing. Go to bed."

It was not like Papa to speak so emphatically, but if she could get him to retire early and sleep, she could save further discussion until another day.

She rolled up the document and stowed it into the hidden compartment and then went to the stack of ledgers on the shelf behind and gathered them up. Finally, she might have a sense of the manor's accounting.

Papa finished with the fire and came and snuffed out her light. "Come along then. You always slept best during a thunderstorm, my brave girl. Your mama used to marvel at it."

"Because I was just like you, Papa."

He chuckled. "Poor dear. She was the only one up all the night worrying."

She didn't have the heart to tell him she would be just like her mother tonight. Mr. Greggson's assault, the plans with their possibility of secret passages, and Papa's revelations about the disputed claim would keep her awake.

"If you don't mind, I'll bring these along for some light reading to aid in falling asleep," she joked. "Perhaps I'll be able to puzzle out the Squire's grocery and candle payments." And his smuggling profits—that was something else she was curious about.

Papa took the stack from her and escorted her to her bedchamber, entering and looking around before handing her the candle. "I know you're not afraid of ghosts, Tilly, and you're not to worry about the Riding Officer, either. I rather hope he does call on me tomorrow. I'll have a few things to say to him."

Not much scared her—she was unimaginative that way. For heaven's sake, the few men who'd taken an interest in her over the years had never frightened her. But she'd never been almost assaulted before, and the incident—and Freddy's rescue—had opened her eyes.

"You must not let him excite you or make you angry, Papa. And be assured nothing happened between us."

Because Freddy had been there. Freddy who, like this house, had secrets.

"I'm not worried. You have always been such a good girl, Tilly. Well-mannered and obedient, in your own way. Your reputation shall prevail over any tale told by the Riding Officer."

Another flash brightened the room like midday and she had a good glimpse of her father's face. He looked grim and determined. He kissed her cheek, wished her goodnight, and left.

He was more concerned than he let on, and he was wrong about her. Well-mannered? Most of the quality thought her too direct, too outspoken. Too common.

She sighed. And obedient? She always tried to cleave to the spirit of the law, but...if a thing needed doing as a matter of justice, well, she would do it.

She understood well why people in need might be tempted by the smuggling trade. Not Sir Richard of course, who'd had land aplenty for his income.

She settled into a chair, took the top ledger from the stack, flipping to the January entries. The column of text ran next to a matching column of numbers. Most entries were clear enough, expenses for food, candles, and clothing.

Others though...she tossed the book aside. It was fanciful to think Sir Richard would have recorded his criminal accounts in with his household expenses.

She built up the fire and went to the window.

Papa had wished her goodnight and told her to lock her door. He'd told her not to go out to the stables for Wulver, but he hadn't commanded her to stay in her bedchamber. She'd barely had time to study those plans.

The wind rattled the windows and a sharp draft sent a shiver through her. Even with the shawl wrapping her, the lavender gown was not as warm as her thick nightgown and heavy robe.

Thunder roared, and she thought of her father, safely abed and sound asleep.

She unfastened her dress and slipped out of it. She could safely roam the halls of Fenwick Manor in her nightclothes and disturb no one but the ghost.

A ghost she didn't believe in.

CHAPTER TWELVE

An hour later, Tilly sat close to the lamp, pouring over the papers spread before her.

During the time she'd changed, made her way to the library, and retrieved the house plans from the hidden drawer, the storm had abated, the rain softening to a steady patter. She'd been relieved to find that Papa had gone to bed and she could study the plans in peace.

Now the storm was deciding to take up its rage again, the lightning and thunder advancing on Fenwick Manor.

She studied the drawing of the library again. The widest space ran along the chimney wall. It made sense that there might be a passage there. Plus, the collection of books on that wall filled only the shelves. Nothing was stacked on the ledges or spilled onto the floor. Of course, one wouldn't want a clutter of books close to the fire, but neither would one want stacked books blocking a secret doorway.

She went to the shelves adjoining the fireplace, examining them. There were no latches or hinges that she could see, and though it seemed just as ancient as the rest of the woodwork, this shelving was unadorned with moldings, unlike the others.

She pushed, trying to rattle the shelves, but they were steady and solid.

The wall of windows and half-shelving behind Papa's desk would not hide a passage so she had only two other choices.

She went to the east wall, shoving aside stacked books and pressing on the small wooden medallions at the corners of shelves. She tugged at the dark wood.

Nothing.

Clutching the parchment in one hand, she crossed to the other wall. This side of the room contained the bound agricultural journals and periodicals saved by generations of baronets, some of them piled on the wide uncarpeted planks in front.

With a sharp crack the room illuminated, the storm gods roared, and she stumbled into a stack.

Paper tumbled about her. She staggered against the shelving, reaching out to steady herself.

A latch clicked. The shelving creaked and inched outward bumping her arm.

Tilly leaned in and peered into a sliver of darkness.

Heart jumping, she breathed in scents—stale dampness, mildew, and ancient wood. If there was human decay, it had dissipated during the past century.

She cinched the belt on her robe, rolled up the plans and jammed them into her bodice. Grabbing the lamp, she felt along the edge of the shelving, tugging. It barely moved.

Shoving more bound journals aside, she set down the lamp. With both hands and every bit of her strength, she yanked at the opening until a spaced widened large enough for her to pass through.

She should go and wake Papa.

But he needed his sleep. He'd looked angry, and tense, and drained tonight when he'd delivered her to her room. She could save this surprise for tomorrow.

Another flash of lightning lit the room and revealed a wall of bare bricks in the passage beyond. No skeleton, no rats, not even a cobweb, though there must be plenty of those.

She tucked the long tail of her plaited hair in with the parchment in the front of her robe, wishing she had thought to wear a cap.

Heart pounding, she tightened her grip on the lamp and inched through the opening. At the last minute, she grabbed a clutch of journals and shoved them into the opening.

A blast of wind gusted. The library panel swung, knocking the journals away.

Panic rose in her. She leaned on the door, managing to shove it open no more than a crack. There was surely a latch on the inside somewhere—those who went in must come out somehow.

The raw wood chilled her cheek as she took a deep breath and peered through the slit. Outside the circle of lamplight, the chasm of darkness rattled her nerves. But she must not panic. If she were to be trapped in this passage, it would only be until morning when Papa rose and returned to his work. He would hear her shouting and tear out the shelving if need be.

She lifted her lamp and studied the space. On this side, the walls were ancient unvarnished planks. The doorway wasn't at all clear.

She set down her lamp and tore a long ruffle from the hem of her nightgown. She jammed it into the small gap she'd created and prayed that a draft wouldn't blow it away.

"Chin up," she said. "If there's one doorway there must be another."

She stepped off the last stair and inched her away along another passage just wide enough for two people.

And how she wished at this moment she wasn't alone.

She'd traveled the short passage outside the library and discovered this circular staircase that wound up and up, surely past the floors of bedchambers and all the way to what must be the attics.

A section of brick loomed, and she placed a hand on it. It was warm. This must be the chimney that reached from the library below, the only room with a fire in this wing of the house.

She moved carefully along, swatting at invisible cobwebs and coughing on dust, until the corridor spilled into a wider space.

Her slippered foot connected with something hard and she stumbled, catching herself on a carved wooden cabinet and lifting her lamp.

Her stumbling block was a trunk. The space was a windowless alcove, accessible only from the passage she'd just traversed, and filled with chests and cabinets.

She grasped the pull on a cabinet door and hesitated, her pulse pounding. This piece of furniture was big enough to contain a skeleton.

Courage. Biting her lip, she eased the door open.

Gowns. Even in such dim light she could discern the rich hues of red, green, gold and purple. She went to another cabinet and found linens. Perhaps these were some of the missing household linens. She circled the room, lifting the lids on a few trunks containing what appeared to be more garments.

In one small wooden chest she found documents. Lifting one to the light, she struggled to read the script. Dated from the last century, it appeared to be a marriage contract.

This must be the muniments room her Papa was looking for, and perhaps some of the Fenwick household items they'd believed stolen were here. What else might she find?

Heart pounding wildly, she remembered the treasure Greggson sought. She should go and wake Papa.

Only one last chest stood against the third wall of the space. This one was locked.

Her pulse quickened, and she studied the ornate keyhole. Surely this was the lock for the last key on her ring.

And drat, she had naught but the key to her bedchamber in her pocket. She hadn't brought the ring of keys. She must go back for them. She must see if the key would fit this lock.

Surely, she could find a way out through the attics that didn't require descending the perilous spiral stairs.

Lifting her lamp higher she circled the alcove again. The walls here were plastered, two of them shortened by the slope of the roof. The third wall was the most likely to have an egress of some sort.

She stretched her arm above the trunk pushed up against it and ran her hand over the bumps and lumps of the ancient plaster. Nothing.

A sturdy cabinet blocked part of the wall. Setting aside her lamp she put all of her weight into it, shifting the heavy cabinet away from the wall.

A netting of cobwebs sent a shudder through her, but no spiders scurried out. But there—a vertical seam broke the expanse of plaster revealing a poorly concealed door. A heart-shaped padlock hung from a metal hasp, the bow of a key sticking out, green with age. Her heart began to pound furiously. She shoved at the cabinet and swatted away the cobwebs.

Grasping the bow, she tried the key. It was stiff as could be.

She took a deep breath and let it out slowly, jiggling the key, praying the metal would not break as she worked it little by little each attempt at a turn.

Finally, with a sharp click, the tumblers rattled, and the lock opened. She slipped the lock off and tugged at the hasp. The door creaked and shifted until she could peek into the space beyond.

A table blocked the entrance. Papers—no, letters were piled there. Beyond the circle of lamplight, she could see nothing.

She pushed the door wider, shifted the letters and set down the lamp.

Letters. In what surely was an unused attic room of Fenwick Manor. She'd visited all the attic rooms. She'd have noticed a pile of letters.

Lightning flashed, and a seam of light pierced a curtained window.

No—she'd visited all the *accessible* attic rooms and none had been curtained. How many more spaces were there like this in the Manor?

She lifted the top letter and studied it. It was no ancient parchment.

Quickly perusing the stack she found three letters addressed to Captain F. G. Sanderford.

Sanderford. She didn't know that name. Did she? It was strangely familiar.

She bit her lip, her stomach going queasy. She should have brought Papa along on this venture, or at least Wulver. Who was F. G. Sanderford? What were his letters doing in her attic?

Spying into another person's correspondence was unthinkable. On the other hand, no one named Sanderford lived at Fenwick Manor. If she hoped to know anything, reading this correspondence was the only logical thing to do, and much more expedient than making inquiries throughout the neighborhood.

She unfolded the top letter and began to read.

> *My dear sir,*
> *I have carefully considered your request and the arguments you've set forth, as well as the difficulties such an endeavor would encounter. I do not say the cause is hopeless, but failing the support of powerful interests, the task will be an uphill battle requiring more evidence than you've submitted. I fear it will be costlier than my previous estimate.*

A chill snaked down her back and she paused. F. G. Sanderford. F.

F as in Frederick? Freddy had been in the army. Under the rough exterior, he knew proper manners. Was he Captain F. G. Sanderford?

Greggson's assertion came to her. He'd been looking for a man...what was the name?

The faintest creak of a step reached her. Her breath caught, and she dropped the letter, stepping back quickly, grabbing the lantern and easing the door closed.

This blasted lamp had no shutter and she dare not risk dousing it. She must somehow find her way back down the stairs, and she'd prefer to not tumble down them in the dark getting there.

Wet and dripping, Freddy slipped through the door of his hut.

He'd dodged the worst of the storm waiting out the rain in a local man's barn, on a night when even the dogs wouldn't bark. He'd still managed to become thoroughly drenched.

He'd made the trip through the secret passages and stairways of Fenwick Manor so many times, he could do it in complete darkness, though anyone wishing to find him could easily track his wet trail. He needed to strip out of these clothes and pray that he didn't shiver himself to death on this bloody cold night. Perhaps with the Squire and his daughter safely abed, he'd take his wet clothes and his wet self and go dry by the kitchen fire.

He pushed open the hidden door of his attic chamber and instantly came alert.

A sliver of light shimmered in the seam of the wall.

His heart clattered. He'd seen no flames from the windows. He'd been all over this house finding every nook and cranny under every eave, and as far as he knew there wasn't one on the other side of this wall. He'd assumed the builders had closed off that space.

If there was a fire... He'd rouse Tilly and her father from their beds, never mind them asking what he was doing there.

He crossed the room and set his palm to the wall. It was as cold as this wet night.

He slid his palm further along, noticed his letter spread out on the table, and pressed against the wall.

The bloody wall moved. He shoved harder and watched the panel swing away from him.

And found himself looking into the astonished face of Tilly Fenwick.

CHAPTER THIRTEEN

"You," she said.

The dark dressing gown leeched most of the light from the lamp in her hand, but a white frill of cloth covered her neck, and a roll of parchment peeked out from the gap in her robe.

His hand itched to explore there, to follow the dark braid that reached from her uncovered hair over her shoulder and down to the gap between two luscious mounds unbound by stays and the other whatnots females used to prop themselves. Wisps of hair had escaped their ribbon and curled wildly about her face. She'd risen from her bed, donned a robe, and found her way into that sealed up space beyond his chamber.

Which hadn't been sealed up at all.

He pushed down his lust and peered at the shadows beyond her. He shouldn't be surprised that Fenwick Manor had another secret room, likely with its own secret passage. But it bloody well bothered him that he'd lodged right next to it and never known.

She leaned in, her mouth tight, and he squashed a smile. Boudicca was getting ready to launch into battle.

He'd never been one to run from an aggressor and as fetching as she looked in her nightclothes, tangling with Tilly would be its own kind of pleasure.

"What the devil are you doing roaming the house at night?" he asked.

She started, her eyes widening, her lamp rising higher.

He clamped a hand over his mouth. She had a netting of cobweb covering her hair.

"*Me*? Roaming the house?" She huffed out a breath. "What are *you* doing roaming about here, in *my* house?" Her eyes narrowed. "Captain F. G. Sanford."

He bit the inside of his cheek swallowing a smile. "If you please, it's Sanderford."

She waved away the correction, as if it didn't signify. "You, sir, have some explaining to do."

He reached out and brushed her hair.

She let out a sharp breath. If he leaned closer, he might have a taste of that luscious sharp mouth.

"Cobwebs," he said, and her hand flew up, raking furiously.

Let me. Her curls had been silky and surprisingly warm. She was a lovely young woman...well, youngish woman. Certainly not older than him.

"What is that room behind you?" he asked.

"I might ask you the same question." She shoved at the table until it bumped him.

"Yes, I suppose you might. Oh, do you wish to enter?" He shifted the table aside. "Please come in, mam'sell."

As her gaze traveled around the room, her face puckered more, and her chest rose and fell enticingly under all that thick wool.

"You're living here," she said, her voice tight.

Never confess. It had been their boyhood motto, his and his brothers'. On more than one occasion, actually on regular occasions, rather than tattle, they'd all taken beatings, one for all and all for one.

She stopped in front of him and glared, putting him in mind of a colonel he'd fought under, one he'd respected.

"Captain Sanderford, I asked you a question."

"Technically, that was a declaration, ma'am."

"Sir," she hissed. Her mouth firmed. "*You* are the ghost."

She jabbed a finger into his chest and the roll of parchment twitched.

He poked back at the parchment. "What do you have here?"

Mouth firming, she grabbed his neckcloth and gasped. "You're sopping wet."

"I was out in the rain."

"In the rain?"

"Yes."

"Why?" She blinked, and another gasp made the parchment twitch. "You went after him?"

He nodded.

"Greggson?" She moved closer. "That was ages ago. What...what did—"

"Nothing happened. I simply followed him to the inn where he lodges."

"Did he know you were following him?"

"I was a soldier in the Canadian frontier. I *do* know how to move about without being seen."

She looked around. "I washed your shirt earlier. It is certainly not yet dry. Have you another change of clothing?"

"I have one more shirt."

"Change into it for heaven's sake."

"In front of a lady," he teased.

"It's too dark for me to see anything."

"I don't wish to compromise you."

"Don't be silly. We're in the two rooms no one else in this house even knows exist."

And didn't that give a man ideas? The sturdy bed in the corner would be big enough for his purposes if seducing Tilly Fenwick might be in the cards.

He slipped out of his coats and stripped off his shirt, watching her. She was chewing her lip, and more hair had slipped out. Even in the dim light, he could see a blush spreading.

And her eyes were cast down, avoiding the sight of his shocking manliness.

He brushed past her and went to the branch of candles, striking the flint until the flames caught.

When he glanced over his shoulder, he found her watching him.

There was boldness in Tilly. There would be heat, also, and sensuality. It would be mixed with an inordinate amount of practicality and loyalty and...caring. Whoever she found herself with would be well-fed and have clean clothing.

Which put him in mind of Greggson. The man would never have Tilly. He would make sure of it somehow.

He fetched his dry shirt, slipped it over his head, and reached for his coats.

"No, Captain. Those coats are wet. Is there no grate in here?"

"No."

"You ought to have chosen better accommodations."

He had, but he'd been required to move when Sir Newton and Tilly arrived. Nor had he expected to still be in residence at the start of a Yorkshire winter.

Tilly pulled a blanket off the bed and draped it around him. "Sit down." She pushed him toward the bed.

"You first, miss," he said.

Her gaze traveled around. The tiny chamber held no chairs.

She sighed and perched on the edge of the mattress.

Freddy settled next to her.

A shiver swept through her and she let out an exasperated breath. "I suppose, if you meant to do Papa and me harm, you would have done so already."

"I would never hurt you or Sir Newton." He reached for her hand and squeezed it.

Her answering tremble passed through her arm and into him.

Outside, the lightning and thunder had died, but the rain slapped the window sharply. Like as not it had had turned to sleet.

He slipped the edge of the blanket over her shoulder and pulled her closer. "You're cold as well."

She angled her head and studied him. "Is there truly treasure here?"

"I don't know."

"Is that why you're here?"

Never confess. Money would be sweet, but it wasn't what he was looking for.

"You would steal it from us?"

It wasn't stealing. If he found money, he would merely be taking back from Sir Richard what was owed, what was needed to save his brother's life.

Digging deep, steeling himself, he gave her the look he'd honed as a young officer, a look he'd used on his most ill-disciplined men, the one he could hold observing a lashing...and for the worst cases, a hanging.

She glared back at him, as fiercely defiant as the worst denizens of the rookeries.

He shook his head and sighed.

"Does anything frighten you?" His hand slipped lower, down her arm and under it, over a slim waist to a generous curve that made his breath—and other parts of him—stir.

"Mr. Greggson's attempt on my person was alarming. I thank you for saving me." A shudder went through her. "Would he have attempted more than a kiss, do you think?"

His fingers moved of their own will, softly stroking. "He's not a man you should be alone with."

"Yes, I do know that. You and my father have both said so. But what about you, Freddy? Ought I to be alone with you?"

He'd never forced a woman, not ever. Not even after the madness of battle had he succumbed to that primitive drive. He'd done his duty to restore order within his men as well.

He'd understood their mad impulses though.

"I *am* a gentleman, Tilly."

She stirred. "Papa...has not been feeling well, I think. I was ever so happy to see him out in the fresh air, but I've worried so about him. Mr. Greggson doesn't know that, but he does know I'm my father's only child. He seeks to coerce me into marriage because he's after the estate and its income, and whatever valuables may be found here, which when Papa dies, he believes will be mine." She let out a minty breath. "But you, Captain Sanderford, you I believe would prefer just money and not my person along with it."

"Tilly—"

"And so, it would probably be wise for you to unhand me."

His hand tightened, bunching the cloth of her robe. "Unhand you?"

She tilted her head and gazed at him, almost an equal in height now that they were sitting. Her lips had parted a fraction and locks of hair draped the deep blue of eyes that glistened in the light from the candles.

"Oh, Tilly." He dipped his head and touched his lips to hers.

Softness. The scents of mint and soap and lilac.

His chest pounded and every nerve in his body roared. She hadn't pulled away, hadn't pushed, hadn't slapped him.

Proceed with caution, he reminded himself. He pressed closer and slanted his lips, coaxing until her mouth opened.

His hand strayed up, under her breast, and he drew her against him.

What, besides parchment, was under the high-necked gowns and the heavy robe? He slid his other hand under the lapel and found her breast, stroking the hard nub.

Tilly gripped his wrist and pulled it away. The glaze in her eyes sent a thrill through him, inciting his lust to attempt more.

The thin press of her lips, however, told him he'd gone too far. He didn't really wish to spend the rest of this frigid night cast into the darkness and freezing in some thin-walled outbuilding. This attic room was cold enough.

Tilly gripped Freddy's wrist and squeezed, her insides quaking. Forget the storm raging outside—a bolt of lightning had just flashed from her breast to that point between her legs.

And she must stop. Here was a man she didn't truly know. What she did know was that he was living secretly in her home, playing a ghost to scare away servants, and he was intent on robbing her.

He pulled his hand loose and tucked a lock of hair behind her ear.

She also knew that his lips were surprisingly soft, that his large hands incited wild feelings in her, and that she didn't mind at all, not really.

"I am a gentleman, Tilly, but I suppose I am only a man first."

A man first...which meant he would do this with any woman.

She pulled her belt tight. "Of course." What a dolt she was.

She tried to stand, but he held both of her shoulders and stopped her. "Let me finish. I am a man, and you are a lovely young woman."

Her heart sunk further. "It was...it was *the kiss* that was lovely." She'd had no idea how kissing would feel. "Do not ruin it with platitudes."

He swiped a hand through his damp hair. "They are not platitudes."

"I'm lovely?" she scoffed. "Young?"

He blinked and his eyes narrowed. "Yes, you are lovely, in a dashing, bold, infuriating way.

And if you're not precisely a girl fresh out of the schoolroom, you're young-ish."

"What?"

He reached around her and lifted her plait. "There's not a trace of gray that I can see here. I should like to undo this and run my fingers through all this loveliness and make sure. And while I'm doing that, I'll watch your eyes darken to midnight blue."

Heat rose in her. She pressed it down and took in a deep breath.

"Do not be ridiculous."

"I'm not. You are a desirable woman, Tilly. And a very good kisser."

She reached around her, searching for the rolled parchment. It had disappeared from her bodice during the kissing. "Now I know you're making fun."

She found the parchment and shoved it back into her bosom.

"I'm not making fun. What have you there?"

He'd moved on from amorous thoughts— *thank heavens.*

"I thank you for that kiss, Captain Sanderford. I confess, it was my first." Perhaps it would be her only, ever.

The thought depressed her.

"I never truly understood how pressing one's lips to a man's could be pleasurable." She wrinkled her nose. "Like Mr. Greggson, ugh."

Freddy frowned, his eyes flitting between the parchment and her lips.

He was a man, he had said, and so he would be capable of dallying with a woman he found mildly attractive. But she also thought he wasn't just distracted by curiosity about the documents she held. A rogue would have satisfied the carnal urge before moving on to satisfy the need for knowledge.

Freddy might be a squatter, a liar, and a potential thief, but there was honor in him. He needed money for a purpose, a purpose that those letters would explain, even if he would not.

She cast off her side of the blanket and a shiver rumbled through her.

Freddy wouldn't likely freeze to death in this attic room, but he might well catch his death from a cold. She saw only the one blanket, and his coats were wet. Even stripped down to bare skin—the image that came to mind sent warmth through her—even then he wouldn't be warm enough.

"You're not staying here." She jumped up, drew him up with her, and tucked the blanket around him. "Pack your things and bring along those candles."

He caught her arm and glared at her. "Are you throwing me out?"

"Don't be silly." She swept up the stack of letters, swatted his hand away when he reached for them, and shoved them into her robe with the parchment. "You're going to tell me the truth, Captain Sanderford, and then we're going to find that treasure together."

Freddy put on his wet coats, gathered up his few personal items and the candles and walked through the hidden doorway.

"We should look here," he said, moving his light to the dark shadows.

"Tomorrow."

"No." He set down his kit and moved around, opening trunks and shuffling through the garments within. He riffled through documents in one trunk—from the last century, nothing recent enough for his search, and fiddled with the latch on a locked trunk before moving to the standing cabinet where he pulled out a rich purple robe and held it up to the light. Gold thread sparkled, stitching the details of an intricate cross.

Tilly gasped. "They're vestments." She moved next to him. "Perhaps it's true that the Fenwicks were Papists." He caught a whiff of her scent as she pressed close. "Perhaps somewhere here is a communion plate and a chalice. If they are gold and bejeweled, *that* might be the treasure. Or...the medieval Bible Papa mentioned might be here."

"You think this is a treasure room?"

She shrugged, her hair tickling his cheek.

Her touch was addling him, or else the dust was constricting his breath.

He hung the gown in the cupboard and swept an arm about her. "Shall we open that locked chest? Have you a crowbar with you?"

She stared up at him, her breath coming in tight gasps. "Of course not."

"Midnight blue again."

"What?"

"Your eyes." He leaned in for a kiss, but she pulled away.

"Don't be a ninny," she said. "We'll come back in the morning with tools." She started off toward a dark passage and suddenly stopped.

"Freddy, how did you access that chamber where you were staying?"

He sighed. "There's a door to the attic corridor. The house is riddled with hidden passages. I thought I'd found them all. How did you enter this room?"

"Through a hidden door in the library."

Bowing, he swept out a hand. "Lead the way, my lady."

She shook her head. "The door closed behind me. I fear I may not be able to open it. It might be better to go your way."

He had spent days sleuthing out his own entrance to the hidden passages of Fenwick Manor. He wasn't ready to reveal all his secrets.

"Together we'll puzzle out how to open that door. And if we can't, I can think of a way we can while away the hours until your father discovers you missing in the morning."

"As long as Edie brings him his breakfast, Father won't notice I'm missing."

"The housekeeper, then, will find us."

She grimaced. "If she returns to work."

"She will. And she's just saucy enough to peep into your bedchamber."

She shook her head and led him out of the alcove.

They squeezed through the narrow passage, the air growing warmer as they passed a chimney. Tilly stopped at the head of a circular staircase.

He drew her aside and examined it. The steps were narrow even on the broadest end, and steep.

"Where does the staircase begin?" he asked.

"On the first floor. I accessed a corridor from the library. The staircase has no other exits for the other floors."

She started off, but he drew her back.

"Allow me."

"Don't be silly."

"If you fall, I'll catch you."

"If I did I'd knock you down the stairs. In any case, I won't fall."

"Nevertheless, allow me to be a gentleman."

She studied him, her eyes shining in the lamplight. "And are you, Freddy? Are you truly a gentleman?"

He touched his nose to hers. "I am, Tilly."

"Oh." She straightened and cleared her throat. "Oh, very well."

At the bottom they arrived at yet another narrow passage. Tilly stopped short next to him. She opened her mouth to speak but a loud thud stopped her.

He put a finger to her lips. "Is it your father?" he whispered.

She lifted a shoulder.

"Where is the door?"

She pointed into the darkness. "I wedged a strip of cloth in the gap."

Her breath tickled his ear as he led her along.

"Wait." She took the lamp and set it upon the floor "No shutter."

Another thud and a muffled curse came to them, the sound growing louder. Tilly moved closer to him.

Some of the manor's passages had not only doors but peep holes as well. He snuffed out his candles and set them aside with her lamp. Then he moved along the wall feeling for gaps of air.

Here. Freddy put his eye to the wall and peeked through.

A shadow crossed in front of him. Whoever it was moved back across the field of vision.

Light shimmered on the hasp of a cutlass and the figure bent over in front of him.

He backed away quickly, pulling Tilly close.

"What—"

He silenced her with a quick kiss and then put his mouth to her ear. "Greggson."

CHAPTER FOURTEEN

Tilly's heart pounded, every nerve in her body quaking, anger rising in her.

The urge to crash through the door and fight was warring with a terrible need to be pulled into the safety of Freddy's arms for another kiss.

Heavens, she mustn't let Greggson intimidate her. What the devil was he doing rummaging in Papa's library?

And...where was Papa?

She pried herself away from the broad chest and put her eye to the spot where Freddy had looked.

Astonishing. The field of vision was narrow, but she could see that a light was bobbing somewhere inside the library.

Was it truly Greggson, or had Papa risen from his bed to work on his manuscript?

The distinctive squeal of the library door came through the wall.

"Papa," she whispered. She clutched Freddy's arm, and he put a finger to his lips. He had his ear to the wall which must simply be the back panel of the bookshelves.

"Well?"

Her breath tightened. Through the peephole, it wasn't hard to hear the conversation within if one paid close attention. That faint gruff voice was definitely not Papa's.

With a shuffle of cloth, a woman crossed her field of vision.

Tilly shivered. She knew this woman. Small in stature, but distinctively large-breasted, she was one of the first maids she'd hired. She'd run out of the house only days ago screaming that she'd seen a ghost. She'd urged all the other servants to run.

What was her name? It would come to her, and she'd track the witch to her home.

Perhaps she'd been one of the housebreakers who'd stolen the manor's household valuables. Greggson's rooms at the inn must be searched.

"They're both fast asleep," the girl said.

"Good."

"You started without me, love?"

Ugh. The girl's seductive oiliness made Tilly's skin crawl.

She'd had a moment's doubt about hiring this one, hadn't she? Hadn't her mother's words popped into her mind—*never hire a flirtatious maid, Tilly.*

Her nails dug into the raw wood of the wall. This was what came of desperation.

"Take that stack over there, Nelda, and go through every book."

Nelda. That was her name.

"You know I can't read."

"You don't need to read to look for loose papers. Bring me any you find."

"Go through every book?" Nelda squawked, her voice rising. "That will take all night. Best just look on the desk. He'll have what you're looking for there. We weren't to touch anything on his desk, plus he was always at work there scratching out his stories when I came in to dust. A charmer he was, much more so than that Long Meg of a daughter."

"Keep your voice down."

Greggson's chastisement had come from the other side of the room, near the windows, where Papa's desk sat.

Tilly rolled away from the peephole and bit down hard on her lip, clenching her fists around the lapels of her robe. Greggson must be seated at Papa's desk pawing through whatever he found in those untidy piles: Papa's journals, his papers, the stories he'd labored over day and night.

How dare he?

Freddy snatched up the lamp and the dead candles, pulled her back toward the staircase and nudged her ahead of him.

"What are you doing?"

"It's time for Fenwick Manor's ghost to appear."

Freddy rushed her up the stairs ahead of him, his face a mask of concentration.

"That mewling voice," he said. "That's Greggson's woman from the inn."

"What?" she huffed. "*That's* his woman? She was one of my maids. She abandoned us."

"She'd come to work here on Greggson's business. I should have paid closer attention."

They'd reached the alcove, and he went straight to a cabinet, rummaging among the clerical robes, retrieving the purple one and then pulling white linens out of a chest.

His words churned in her. "You drove the servants away. Intentionally."

"Come along." He tugged her into his chamber, stopping to pull a dagger from under one end of the mattress, and a pistol and powder bag from the other and stuffing them into the waist of his trousers.

"Mightn't we just run in and hold them at gunpoint?"

"Let's try this way first. Let's fluster them first. I don't want you or your father hurt."

"I ought to be furious with you."

He took her hand and smiled. "But I'm glad you're not."

His grin touched a place in her heart, stirring emotions she'd never experienced. She *should* be angry, but she wasn't. Couldn't be.

His hand came up to caress her cheek. "There's naught like going into battle with a stout-hearted comrade by one's side. Come."

Heart roiling, she followed him through an egress into the main attic corridor and stopped at the next hidden doorway.

He turned her to face him.

"I should blindfold you," he said.

She scoffed. "It's my house."

He eyed her up and down, a slow grin forming. His lips touched hers, sending her heart pounding wildly. She fell into him, parting her lips, praying he wouldn't stop.

When he pulled her head to his shoulder, she wanted to weep.

"We must stop," he said. "Your father—"

"Might awaken." How could she have forgotten? "Let's go then. Show me the way."

He put a finger under her chin and eased it up. "I'm revealing my secrets. But I'm holding you to your contract. We'll find that treasure together."

His gaze held none of his usual humor. It was serious, almost...haunted. This way out of his chamber was the least of Freddy Sanderford's secrets, nor his troubles. He had more, but he would not have to contend with them alone.

"Our contract says you will have to share all your secrets, but for now, what are we waiting for? I want to see the ghost of Fenwick Manor in action."

She followed him through a complicated series of dark passages and hidden staircases that made her head spin, finally popping through a swinging cabinet into the kitchen.

Wulver struggled up from slumber and came over to nose them. "You were meant to be in the stables. How...oh never mind." She set down the candles and lamp and fondled the dog's ears. "It's certain they didn't come in this way. Even in the hidden passages, we would have heard Wulver announcing them."

Freddy was biting his tongue and frowning.

"How did they enter?" she asked.

He turned away and tossed the rumpled clothing items over a chair, shedding his wet coats.

"You know of other ways to enter."

"The flame of his candle was flickering. I imagine he scaled the ivy and came in the library window then let her in the front door."

"I closed the window."

"Is the latch solid?"

"I...I don't know." Perhaps that was why it was always open. The wind blew it open and Papa never noticed.

He lifted the white garment he'd brought from the alcove, shaking it out and sending dust motes flying.

"It's an alb." She fingered the cloth. "Of quality cloth."

"Must be, since it's lasted this long." He slipped it over his head and tugged.

With a sharp squeal, the cloth rent down the back.

Tilly let out another tight breath. He would rip the ancient garment to shreds. It was almost a sacrilege. "Papa has one that would fit you better."

He squirmed, and another split tore.

"Stop struggling." She worked the cloth over his arms. "I hope the old priest doesn't appear to chastise us."

"Not a chance," he said.

The cloth didn't cover Freddy's long legs. His damp trousers outlined strong, muscled calves. She tore her gaze away.

"The priest was shorter than you and less, er, broad in the shoulders."

"This will do for our purposes. This purple robe might cover the gap."

He pulled the purple vestment over his head.

Tilly stepped back, studying him, smoothing her hand over the silver embroidery. "This garment is called a chasuble." Someone stitched this centuries ago, a nun perhaps, or a Catholic lady, one with the leisure time for such a large piece of work. With each reverent touch, she felt the past pulling her in. She could almost believe in ghosts.

A large hand came down over her own.

"You are stroking my chest, Tilly, and it's stirring an urge to forget about Greggson."

Heat flamed in her cheeks. Greggson. Of course. They must hurry. The priest wouldn't mind them using his garments to dispense with a villain and his harlot.

"Is this how you'll appear? Greggson will know it's you."

He strolled off to a sideboard and fumbled in the dark, splashing water and rattling dishes, and returned with the round silver platter they'd used for the fish.

"What will you do with that?"

"I'll be holding the Eucharist aloft for adoration."

"*Good heavens.*"

"What?" He peered down at her. "Too sacrilegious?"

"If there really were Papist bones in these walls, this would stir them to vengeance."

He dropped a kiss on her forehead. "It's in a good cause."

"I suppose. What am I to do?"

"Follow me."

Freddy tucked the platter under his arm, handed her the lamp, and led the way to the inner door that opened to the servant's staircase.

"Why not go back through the secret passage?"

He shushed her and opened the door, nudging her through.

Wulver shoved her nose into the gap, and Freddy caught her just in time, pushing her back.

"No, old girl. You'll stay here. They know who you are. They won't dash away in fear of you and I won't see you hurt."

Freddy shoved the door on the dog who promptly whimpered.

He touched her shoulder, breathing into her ear. "While I proceed to the library, you wake your father and bring him along there."

"Then he'll discover you're here. He'll winkle it out that you've been living under his eaves."

The light from the lamp cast shadows on Freddy's face and amplified the intensity of his gaze. "Were you going to keep my secret from him, Tilly?"

Her toes curled in her slippers and a wriggle of anticipation raised the hair on her neck. She shook it off. "I could never." Papa should know who was living under his roof, and knowing him, he would have her hauling in ticking for a better guest chamber for his unwanted guest.

"I didn't think you could."

Guilt nagged at her. She'd prefer Papa not know about the kissing. "Shall I have my father bring a weapon?"

"I am armed."

"Under your vestments. You'll never reach your pistol in time. Nor did I see you load it."

He sent her a sharp look and then smiled. "You are damned observant, Tilly."

"Language, sir."

"I'll go into battle with you any time."

Her heart did a little flip. "I'll be right behind you."

He dropped a kiss on her forehead. "But not tonight. You're correct that Greggson is armed, and not likely to be fooled by the sight of a ghost. I'm counting on the maid to raise a ruckus and distract him. We'll wrap him up tight before your father rouses from sleep and turn the bastard over to the new local justice of the peace." He handed her the platter, yanked up his skirts and hastily loaded his weapon.

"How will you carry your pistol? You've no coat to stow it under."

"I'll hold it in my hand."

"And your knife?"

"In the waist of my trousers."

"Hard to reach in a hurry."

He placed the pistol on a step and ripped the side of the chasuble and then the undergarment.

She gasped.

He arranged his garments, retrieved the pistol, and leaned into her ear again, inhaling her clean scent. "Needs must, my love. Besides, you brought it up."

Warmth shot through her. *My love.* He'd called her his love.

On the other side of the door, Wulver's whines had turned into a menacing grumble.

"Wulver has finally sensed the intruders," she whispered.

"Or she may just be annoyed she's missing the adventure."

"She'll start barking soon. We must hurry."

He followed her noiselessly, and when they reached the library floor, she touched his hand. "Careful," she whispered.

As she moved down the corridor to the other wing, she turned back to look. Freddy had extinguished the lantern, but a bright flash of lightning through the window below shimmered on the upraised platter.

A sharp bark and a howl from the kitchen pierced the air, followed by a thud as heavy as distant thunder. Wulver might well crash through that doorjamb and rush up to join in the battle.

Which might not be a bad thing.

She hastened down the corridor to Papa's bedchamber.

Tilly clutched the lamp and raced up the single flight of stairs and along the corridor to Papa's door. She grasped the latch and pushed. It was locked.

The girl had said she'd found Papa asleep. Might she have stolen a key when she worked for them?

Belowstairs, Wulver barked again.

Tilly scratched at the door and called out. No answer.

Nelda said she'd found Tilly fast asleep as well. She might have peeked into the dark chamber and mistaken the gown she'd left on the bed.

She ran down the corridor and rattled her latch. It was still locked.

Or Nelda might have lied.

Wulver sent up an eerie howl like the banshee of death, and Tilly's teeth began to chatter.

She couldn't let Freddy face Greggson alone. She didn't have time to unlock her chamber, get her ring of keys and go back to Papa's room. Let him sleep.

She picked up her skirts and ran.

CHAPTER FIFTEEN

·

Thud. Yowl. Thud. Yowl.

Freddy measured his steps approaching the closed library door, timing them with the thuds of Wulver flinging her beastly self against the door.

A panicked squeaking leaked through the library door panel, matched by a male murmuring.

Thud. Thud.

Crash.

The dog's nails *tap-tap-tapped* up the steps. On the other side of the door, the squeaking and murmuring came closer. He swallowed an inappropriate chuckle and let it rumble up again in a fearful moan, the silver platter raised just high enough that he could see under it.

The door latch clicked. He let out a long painful groan, as if the Lord Protector's executioner had just extracted his guts.

Dark fur whizzed past, knocking him aside, and then a flurry of dark robes flew by, knocking his pistol away. Wulver growled and a woman shrieked.

"You," Tilly yelled.

The bellow that followed was distinctly a man's.

He hurried in. Greggson had Tilly by the arm, and she was battling him valiantly with kicks and punches while he swatted at the dog who was clamped on his leg.

In two strides he was on the man. He brought the heavy platter down on his head.

Greggson rolled, kicked the dog away, and reached for his pistol. Tilly kicked at him, sending the shot wild and knocking over a stack of books. Freddy bashed him again with the platter and tossed it aside, using his fists.

They fought then, wildly, the dog bouncing between them. When Greggson landed a kick on the dog, sending her squealing, Tilly's scream tore his attention away. The maid was escaping through the window, swatting at the dog who had rallied to get a grip on her skirts.

"Help me, Basil," she shouted.

With a large rip, she fell from the window, and Wulver flew back, a hunk of cloth clamped in her jaws.

"What are you doing here, Greggson?" Tilly shouted.

He turned to see the villain's blade pointing at Tilly.

He grabbed the ladder-back chair near the squire's desk, and flung it, knocking the blade out of Greggson's hand, then dug through the slit in his gown for his own weapon.

Greggson righted himself, the dagger flew, and Greggson dove for the window.

The damp chill licked his cheeks as he watched the Riding Officer limp off.

Tilly joined him at the window, her breath coming in tight gasps. "I see you, Mr. Greggson. You wait until my father hears about this. I'll see you arrested."

He gripped her shoulders, pulling her back and looking her over. "Let's keep you out of his range. Greggson generally carries two pistols." There were no obvious injuries but the darkness of the heavy wool would hide blood.

She put a hand to his cheek. "You're injured."

When he touched his tongue to the corner of his mouth, he tasted blood. "A minor cut. Are you all right, Tilly?"

He smoothed his palms over her body and she gasped.

Her dressing gown was dry, thank goodness. "That hurt?"

"No. I'm not hurt," she said, lifting his hand away. "Don't be a nodcock."

He reached for her arms holding them loosely. "Me, a nodcock? I was meant to go in first and alarm them. What were you doing?"

"As if he would believe that ridiculous ghost story." Tilly peered out the window and then leaned over the sill. "Even Nelda. Her sighting when she was in my employment was only a ruse to drive out all my staff so Greggson—"

She looked up at him, her eyes narrowing.

"No." He shook his head. "She wasn't working for me. Greggson must have made more forays into the house, though I confess I only saw him here once before."

She gasped. "This great blasted house. Can I ever feel safe here?"

That thread of shame twisted in him again. "I'll make sure of it."

"And you're assuming you'll be staying on here." She poked her nose out the window again. "It's a long way down. Nelda will have twisted something I hope."

"Greggson was limping."

"Good. I hope he's broken a bone, the vile—" She huffed out a breath. "I must see to Papa. His door was locked. The noise should have woken him."

A trembling started in her. He drew her close and her wriggling sent his heart pounding.

"Or—should we should go after them?" she squeaked.

Thunder crashed, the sudden streak of lightning accompanying it illuminating the landscape below, and the skies opened. "It's pouring again." And Farnsworth had warned him off the Riding Officer tonight. "Come. Does your great ring of keys have one for your father's bedchamber?"

She huffed out a breath.

"I saw it the first day I met you."

She sighed, picked up her skirts, and hurried out, the dog rushing after her.

"Wait," he called.

But she was already gone.

He should follow her. She and her father had taken rooms in the new wing of the house, which rooms he didn't know.

But while she ran off to her father's room, he had a chance to retrieve weapons, and more importantly to search. Earlier when he'd lit the way for Greggson's tour, he'd blocked the Riding Officer's view of what looked like a stack of ledgers on the shelf behind the squire's desk.

He'd been looking for them—Sir Newton must have brought them with him. Those books were as good a place as any to look for evidence of the Riding Officer's bribes.

And now they were gone.

Greggson had left empty-handed, of that he was almost certain.

He picked up the Riding Officer's candle and surveyed the room. Books lay about everywhere in front of the stacks, but one pile caught his eye. One set of shelves jutted out, and he felt around the molding until he found the latch and eased the opening wider.

Clever, clever girl to have found this in all this disarray. He counted out the shelving units, marked the location of the latch in his memory, and shoved the door closed.

He was picking up the chair when Tilly rushed in, panting.

"Papa is gone," she said. "I'm going after Greggson."

Are you mad? He went to her and pulled her into his arms.

"Could he be somewhere else? Another bedchamber perhaps?"

"No." Her curls tickled his cheek as she shook her head, filling him with her scent.

"Might he have gone out on his own?"

"At night? In this weather?" She stepped out of his embrace and paced the room. "Well, perhaps. It's not impossible. Wulver was in the stables. If he brought her into the house—we should look in the stables." She paused and covered her face with her hands. "What if he was assaulted by Greggson and left there, or outside somewhere?"

It wasn't impossible. The stableboy might be Greggson's.

"We'll look." He closed the window and struggled to latch it.

"Papa keeps it always open. I'd closed it when I was in here earlier."

The lantern illuminated the desktop with the scattered papers.

"Greggson was going through these. Papa's things are never in this sort of jumble. Oh, Papa."

"Steady, my girl. I doubt Greggson has your father. Not if he sent Nelda to his chamber to find him. And Nelda reported that you and Sir Newton were safe in your beds."

"Both our doors were locked, and his bed was never slept in."

"Nelda lied."

"Unless she has keys."

She might, but he doubted it. Greggson would have been running about the manor at all hours if his doxy had keys.

"Might your father have gone out?" he asked again. Farnsworth had been out and about tonight. What were the chances he and Sir Newton were together?

Tilly reached for the lantern. "Stay here if you wish, but I'm going to go look for him. What if he's wondered off in search of a ghost story? What if he's gone to that blasted glen? Come, Wulver."

"Tilly, wait." He yanked the garments over his head and shivered.

"You're freezing. Stir the embers, and you can wait here."

"And where exactly are you going?"

"To the stables, and then...I don't know. I must find my father."

He took the lantern from her. "Not without me."

*****

While the stable boy yawned and rubbed at his eyes, Tilly's jaw and her fists worked, clenching and unclenching.

Freddy's own patience was wearing thin. "Well?" he asked.

"Squire came for the horse a good while ago." The lad's frown slid to the corner where Wulver was sniffing. "Took the beast with him as well."

Tilly made a scoffing noise.

"No, he didn't," Freddy said. "He put the dog in the house." No doubt the squire had been thinking of Tilly's protection, and damn foolish it was, considering that Greggson had invaded the library while he was out running around the county.

Though in all fairness, Sir Newton wouldn't have known that Greggson was planning to invade his library, would he?

Where the devil had Tilly's father gone?

Freddy rounded on the boy. "Did you see anyone else about?"

The boy glared back. If he was wondering why a manservant was squeezed into an ill-fitting greatcoat that belonged to the squire accompanying the lady of the house—and she in her nightclothes—well, he could just keep wondering.

"Answer the man, Max," Tilly said.

"No." The lad shook his head. "Didn't see no one."

Freddy glanced at Tilly. "A double negative. When did the Squire leave?"

"'Twas a good while ago."

"Yes," she spluttered. "You've said that already."

He stopped under the overhang. Damnation, in the short trip across the yard to the kitchens, she'd get as soaked as himself.

"This will ease up in a moment," he said.

"While we freeze to death." She shook off his grip and grabbed his hand. "It's already turning to sleet. Come on."

They ran through the puddles and rivers of freezing mud to the kitchen entrance, the dog darting past them.

Water ran down her cheeks, and what remained of her plait hung in limp tendrils. He returned the squire's greatcoat to a hook, grabbed a shawl and patted her face.

"Look at us. You're soaked and I've ruined another coat." He dropped the shawl around her shoulders. "Let's get this kitchen fire going."

"No."

Freddy's gentle patting had muddled her brain, but she knew she couldn't sit around in these wet garments, not even before a roaring kitchen hearth. She was heartily sick of this night, sick of the weather, and worried—*sick*, in fact—about Papa.

He'd catch his death in this storm and die, and then where would she be? Oh, she'd have a home, a great blooming monstrosity of a home, and whether she could generate income to sustain it was anyone's guess.

The smell of damp wool and Papa's soap and another scent she recognized as Freddy's own— *good heavens*—rose around her while shivers and trembles were starting in her bones. She had to get out of this clothing. And if *she* was miserable, he must be so twice over having got himself thoroughly drenched twice in one night.

He needed dry things as well. Papa had more than one heavy banyan, and she would find it.

"Come." She took his hand again, conscious of his strength, aware that he was going along with her, following her lead.

And where was she leading him?

Wulver flew through the house with them— since the kitchen door jamb was completely broken away. Another repair to be made.

As they reached the floor where her father's and her bedchamber stood at opposite ends of the corridor a fierce trembling seized her and Freddy's arm came around her. "Which room is yours?" he asked.

Her breath caught. "You don't know?"

"No."

"You haven't been peering into my bedchamber through some secret peephole?"

"Heavens no. If there's a passage in this wing, I haven't found it. We must look at your map of the building."

The map. When she'd run for her key to her father's room, she'd shoved the house plans and Freddy's letters under her bed—admittedly not the best of hiding places, but expedient, and dry. This rain would have ruined the documents.

She left Wulver to patrol the corridor while Freddy hurried behind her into her father's bedchamber. She snatched up a banyan and turned to see him peeling off his shirt.

This time she had a glimpse of his chest, as astonishing a revelation as the wide shoulders and back she'd seen earlier. A smattering of dark hair covered an expanse of muscles that flexed as he shook out the garment he'd been wearing. Freddy hadn't been some soft staff officer, sitting around drinking brandy. He was a man powerfully built, a man who had done physical work. A man who could throw a formidable punch.

Air whooshed from her, making her giddy. Alone in the manor with Freddy, the danger was palpable. And she wanted to dive in.

CHAPTER SIXTEEN

"What are you d-doing?"

Papa would see the shirt and wonder why it was here and why it was wet. He would only have to look at her and she would spill out all the events of the evening, including the interlude in the attic.

But it had only been a kiss.

Only a proper kiss, one that had made her arms and legs and toes and other parts of her tingle as they never had before. She wasn't opposed to having more kisses like that if she but dared.

She wasn't prepared to tempt Papa to question her, not just yet, and not until he'd explained his own absence.

"Not over that chair," she said. "You'll drip everywhere and ruin the carpet, and it's cold in here." The way Papa liked it. She found the banyan and held it while he shrugged into it. "Come with me." She grabbed the sopping shirt.

Again, Freddy complied, crowding his naked chest into her at the door to her bedchamber. She pulled out her ring of keys.

"Your door was locked also?"

"As I said."

"So Nelda did lie. She never entered your chamber."

"Unless there's another way in."

She flung the shirt over a chair and crossed to the fireplace, poking at the banked embers until Freddy nudged her aside and knelt to arrange firewood.

"I watched you the other day chopping this." His lopsided smile made gooseflesh rise, and when he got to his feet and took both of her hands, her cheeks burst into flames. "I'm sorry, Tilly. I should have gone out and completed the task for you."

She managed a breath. "You shouldn't have conjured rumors of the ghost who drove away my man chopping the wood."

The kindling caught, sending a fresh gust of warmth and inciting a shiver in her.

Or maybe his closeness had caused that. Her breath came in short spurts and she trembled more.

Freddy frowned. "You're freezing."

The belt of her robe slackened and fell open. He spun her around and yanked the sopping garment from her.

She heard a sharp intake of breath behind her and glanced down. Her wet nightgown was all but transparent.

"I've turned around," he said. "Though I confess you are a lovely woman, Matilda Fenwick, and I would prefer to look my fill. And I'm also perfectly willing to help you out of your nightdress."

Heart pounding fiercely, she looked over her shoulder. He had in fact turned around.

His offer to undress her made more warmth uncurl in her. She was a country girl. She knew about breeding. She knew what went on between a man and a woman. The marital act, mother had called it, explaining things. The way she'd described, it hadn't seemed pleasant.

But Freddy's kiss—this was a chance she might never have again.

Though what did she know about Freddy's family and character and past? Nothing really.

She hastened to a dark corner of the room and rummaged in her clothespress.

She tore off the wet nightgown and fumbled into a dry one, barely able to breathe. Wrapping herself in an oversized shawl, she fetched a dry towel and returned to the fire.

"All finished?" he asked.

Temptation weighed on her. She gulped in air, fighting for control.

He glanced over his shoulder and lifted his head, sniffing the air like Wulver and grinning. "Lemon and lilac," he said.

"Excuse me?"

"Your scent."

The scented oil was her own creation, a bit of vanity that gave her pleasure. But the fact that he'd noticed, and his playful grin, meant she had to fight harder for self-control. She handed him the towel. "Here. Remove the rest of your wet clothing and dry yourself."

The light from the fire sparkled in his eyes. "*All* of my wet clothing?"

Must not smile. Must not. She drew herself up and raised an eyebrow. "Freddy. I'm being practical. I cannot have two ailing men under my roof to look after."

"And you would look after me, wouldn't you?"

"Of course, I would. It would be my...my Christian duty."

There. Her voice had shook only a little. Had that been convincing?

A long gaze followed, one that heated her more than the fire. Thoughts of attending Freddy in his bed—not the meager cot in the attic, but a proper bedchamber—sent another thrill through her, but she held his gaze calmly, or as calmly as possible. Finally, he went off to the dark corner.

She turned back to the flames. The wood crackled and spit, small puffs of steam streaming up. She had, in fact, cut this wood, and carried it in multiple trips up to her room, up to her father's library, up to his bedchamber.

Papa. She must concentrate on Papa, on his health and his safety. She would make a home for them, by God, a place that would be Papa's and hers, and hers alone when he was gone, a place to grow roots.

To grow a family? Oh, how she would love that.

But she would not love a husband like Mr. Greggson. He'd marry her, take everything, and ruin everything. He was more likely to give her the pox than a passel of children.

Freddy...oh what did she truly know about him? He might do the same.

His scent signaled his return, and she closed her eyes, fighting more shivers. She must snap out of this. She must think.

"Shall we look at those plans?" he asked.

Tilly let out a long breath, glad that one of them was being business-minded. "Yes."

And then she made the mistake of looking at him again.

Tingles zinged through her fingers and toes, and tendrils of heat curled everywhere else, settling at the juncture of her legs. He'd filled the shoulders of Papa's banyan to bursting, leaving a long gap in the front, an arrow of that muscled chest that made her quiver.

"Tilly?" he said.

She fanned herself and looked around. Her room had no proper table, only the small bedside stand where she'd placed the ledgers. The only viable flat surface was the bed.

Freddy's gaze followed the line of her own.

"I'll get them," she said, voice cracking.

She retrieved the rolled documents and dropped to her knees on the worn Turkey carpet. "Bring the light over please."

He set the lamp on the planked floor near her. "It's blasted hard to see."

She watched his stockinged feet moving around, wondering if he'd truly removed his trousers or kept them on.

And that way lay madness. Freddy Sanderford—Captain Sanderford to her—was a man fallen on hard times, a squatter who wanted something from Fenwick Manor. That something would never be the squire's spinster daughter.

She ought to remember that. She ought to find out what he really wanted, besides some imaginary treasure.

She forced her gaze back to the lines laid out before her.

"More light." Freddy placed a candle near her.

For the umpteenth time this night, his breath tickled her ear.

It was impossible to concentrate around him. She was as addlepated as the greenest girl in the village. The lines jumbled together, all the rooms drawn there, the small and large and in-between, all looked alike on the page.

Her hands shook tracing the inked patterns. "I can't make heads or tails of this."

Did he know how nervous he made her? His shoulder bumped hers.

"Look here." One calloused but clean finger landed upon the paper. "The corridor. Then we have one, two, three, and four doors—we are here, you and I, in your bedchamber."

Oh, he'd infused that remark with promises. Taking in a careful breath and letting it out slowly, she retrieved some of her good sense. "Yes. Now I see. And these walls—they aren't drawn thickly enough to contain a passage it seems."

"Thank heavens. I shouldn't like anyone creeping about spying into your bedchamber. I would wall up any such entries like I did the sheep pen." His hand smoothed the paper, moving up the page to the outline of the building's opposite wing. "This other wing seems to be a full century older than the one we are in. You chose to sleep in the more modern part of the house."

Modern? She wrinkled her nose. "They are both equally mildewed and dry-rotted." She set a finger to a corner of the plan where the uppermost floors were depicted. "Here is the area in the old wing where your attic room and the alcove should be, shown as empty space under the eaves."

"And here." He poked the paper. "Sir Richard's bedchamber is on the floor in between, but down the corridor from the library."

"And that is the route you use to visit the kitchens."

"Yes." His finger traced from the kitchen to the attic until he touched hers.

Tingles sparked through her hand, like being licked by the flames on Guy Fawkes day. And she couldn't make herself pull away.

"Tilly." He breathed out her name. Trembling, she turned her head and welcomed his lips.

Softness. Freddy's lips touched gently, carefully, tenderly, drawing her to him, and she found herself demanding more. She caressed the back of his neck, steadying herself and parting her lips for the touch of his tongue. Her shawl slipped as her other hand moved to the scratchy wool of his banyan's lapel. Straightening up on her knees she accepted his warm hand on her breast and arched to meet him.

His touch was tender, and wicked, and she *shouldn't.*

When he kissed her neck, pleasure shot through her. She shoved away scruples. Why not allow this with Freddy? He wanted her, not Fenwick Manor.

Surrendering, she let him ease her down onto the carpet.

Downstairs, a door slammed, and in the hallway, Wulver *woofed.*

Could it be Papa? Freddy tilted his head, listening.

Besides the *woof*, the only sound was the beat of her heart, and the rasp of her tight breaths. He must think her a wanton. Heavens, she *was* a wanton.

She glanced down. Freddy had untied the neck of her nightdress and he cradled her bared breast.

The quivering started again, shooting up and down and up again.

She looked up into dark eyes. His mouth went slack, his gaze sharpened, and he squeezed her breast gently, flicking his thumb over the nub.

Pleasure roared through her, making her gasp.

Woof.

Freddy blinked and his hand stilled. "I'd best investigate that."

When he took his hand away, cold rushed her, and she tugged at her bodice. "I'll go with you."

"You'll do no such thing."

She snatched up her shawl and pulled it around her. "Of course, I will. This is my house."

"I'll not have you in danger."

"I can say the same thing."

"And what if it's your father returning?"

He would understand. Surely, he would. She let out a breath. "It's probably the broken door. But if it is him, I'll explain everything."

"Everything about why I'm alone with you in your bedchamber, you in a nightdress and me naked under his banyan?"

She closed her eyes on that image. "You're not naked. You're wearing your trousers."

"Ah, you looked." Grinning, Freddy stood, and she wobbled up as well and followed him to the door. As soon as he opened it, Wulver rushed in, heading for the fire.

Tilly ran to retrieve the lamp, candle and papers before the dog set them all ablaze.

"Don't go investigating without me," she called.

He stuck his head out into the corridor, peered around, and then closed the door, turning the key in the lock.

"I believe Wulver just wanted to come in. Now, where were we?"

She hugged the shawl closer and pushed the dog away with her foot. "Page two. The grounds and outbuildings."

From the chair by the fire, Freddy watched Tilly's chest rising and falling in time with the dog's snoring. She'd shown far less interest in the plans of the grounds and outbuildings, which were imprecise at best. The structure that housed his own secret entrance was not even on the map—likely there were more passages and places stored away in the brains of the locals who used the secret caves and passages for their warehousing.

In repose, she looked vulnerable, soft, and warm. He was having a devil of a time trying not to touch her. Touching her was dangerous—if not for the dog, he might have proceeded directly to tupping her, he who had nothing to offer. He'd never ruin her and force a marriage, like some beggarly scoundrel—like Greggson.

Thanks to the beast, he'd stepped away, and they'd talked, and talked, and talked, Tilly yawning and recounting tales of her father and his inclination to run out into the night chasing a good story. She'd agreed that Sir Newton must surely have stayed the night with Farnsworth.

At Gorse Point Cottage? Perhaps, but it might just as well be some other haunt that Farnsworth knew of.

Farnsworth worked for the Crown. He and the Earl of Shaldon, who most believed ran the Crown's network of spies, were as thick as thieves. Farnsworth had chased Freddy away from the Riding Officer, and then he'd come back for Sir Newton, and then Greggson and the inn girl had invaded this house. And no one had returned.

He mulled over the possibilities. The weather must have kept the luggers out at sea, else surely Greggson would have scampered off after the men waiting to offload cargo.

Except that, Greggson might have taken someone's coin to stay away.

He raked his fingers through his hair. Surely Sir Newton had only been playing the ghoul-hunting fool for the neighborhood. He'd misled his daughter as well. But why had he allowed Greggson a tour of the library? Had he planted something there for the Riding Officer to find? Perhaps he wanted to tempt the man to return.

A chuckle bubbled up. Sir Newton's enthusiasm for ghosties, goblins, and ghouls seemed genuine, and what could be more nightmarish than a visitation by Basil Greggson?

Tilly stirred, lifted her head, and looked around squinting. "You're still here. I...I fell asleep. How did I..."

"After you passed out in the middle of a sentence, I deposited you in your bed."

She glanced down and yanked the covers up to her neck.

Freddy swallowed another laugh. Removing her shawl had allowed him another good look at her lovely person. In other circumstances, he'd ask for her hand, and willingly.

But he had nothing to offer the lass, and he'd veered too far from his purpose. As long as tonight would be their secret, she wouldn't be ruined.

Though if he was looking to get leg-shackled— and he wasn't—he'd never find a better partner than Tilly.

"You've dressed. Your clothes can't possibly be dry."

"I took the liberty of borrowing another of your father's clean shirts."

Tilly gasped. "Papa." She sat up and swung her legs off the bed.

"He hasn't returned. I popped into the library, and there's no one about in there. The thud we heard earlier was the wind slamming that broken kitchen door. Or perhaps it was a ghost. In any case, there are no fleshly visitors lurking about. And you should go back to sleep."

"Where could he possibly be?" She pressed back a yawn.

Freddy rose and drew closer, holding back a smile when she started to stand up.

"What are you doing?"

"Tucking you back in bed."

He lifted the blanket, and she scooted back, giving him a glimpse of shapely calves and slim feet. And he'd seen enough of her in the wet gown to know that the rest of her was all well-rounded loveliness. And by god the girl could kiss.

A buzzing started between his ears and moved down to his chest as he dropped the blanket over her. Plopping down next to her he pushed the covers under her chin.

Her hand crept out and sought his. His heart tightened as her grasp firmed.

"He is safe with Lord Farnsworth?"

"Yes. And you said he's always come home unharmed when he's gone off on a jaunt."

"Yes." She gave his hand a squeeze. "You'll help me find him."

"If need be."

She nodded, frowning. "And then you'll tell me why you're here and what you're looking for. Papa and I will assist you. I promise you that."

She struggled up onto her elbow, pulled his hand to her mouth for a kiss, and gazed at him for a long moment.

With her hair tangled about her shoulders, and plump parted lips inviting him to take more, she looked like a woman in need of a tumble.

And he was just the man for it. Somehow, he'd get there, but not here, not now.

He let out a long breath. That had been a foolish thought. He'd never do anything to ruin Tilly's chances at marriage.

He kissed the fingers wrapping his own, and set them down.

Wulver came over and rested her chin on his knee, staring soulfully until he found the spot on her head needing scratching.

As Tilly drifted off, the first dim rays of dawn slipped through the curtains and cast a light on the bedside table.

Freddy nudged the dog away and reached for one of the books resting there. He studied the line of notations and figures.

His heart pumped harder, the fog in his head clearing. He swept up the stack of books and went back to the chair and the candle.

Sir Richard's accounts were sloppily kept by a man who cribbed letters and numbers like a child in the schoolroom, except for one book, undated but carefully notated.

He shoved it into his waistband. This was the book Basil Greggson—B. G. in Sir Richard's notations—was looking for. Amazing that a criminal mastermind like Sir Richard would keep such careful records of his bribes.

Tilly awoke with Wulver stretched next to her.

It was light outside, the gray light signaling mid-morning. The fire in the grate glowed, as though someone had built up a grand fire not so many hours ago.

Freddy. She pulled the covers up around her. Freddy had done that. He'd tucked her in. He'd kissed her hand—her hand, and not her head or her cheeks, or her lips.

And then she'd fallen asleep watching him lavish the dog with affection.

She fell back into the pillows. Two kisses…no, it had been at least three, three proper kisses she'd experienced with Freddy.

She'd almost had another—with Greggson. *Ugh.*

And Papa might still be missing. The events of the previous night rushed back to her: the dinner, Greggson's attempt on her person, Freddy's rescue, the hidden staircase, the muniments room with its treasures, and Freddy's secret hideaway, Greggson and Nelda in the library, more hidden staircases…

And those kisses. Those smoldering, heart-melting kisses.

Wulver lifted her head and thumped her tail.

Tilly kissed the dog's ear, then leaped out of bed, throwing on a gown and snatching her ring of keys from near the stack of ledgers on the bedside table. If Papa had returned, she must show him the passage and room she'd discovered.

And the house plans…she glanced around the chamber. The rolls of parchment they'd studied together rested safely upon the mantel.

Freddy hadn't taken them.

But what of his letters? Those she hadn't yet read. She ducked down to peer under the bed. Freddy hadn't taken those either.

Had he seen where she'd hid them? Did he want her to read them?

First, she must find Papa. She shoved the letters into her pocket.

CHAPTER SEVENTEEN

In the kitchen, Edie scowled up from the washbasin.

The cook stood nearby, drying dishes, all of her jowly wrinkles screaming annoyance. Tilly let Wulver out the back door and fetched a teapot.

"Have you seen Sir Newton?" Tilly asked.

Edie shrugged. "Did he not go off with your new footman? Him who was supposed to do all the washing up last night."

"Was he? I hope you reached your homes before the worst of the storm. Have you seen either of them?"

Edie harrumphed.

She set down the teapot. "Edie. Rose. Where is Sir Newton? Did you see him? Did he go off with the, er, footman? Did *either* of you see *either* of them?"

"No one's come through," the cook said, "nor called for breakfast."

Edie shook her head and muttered about footmen who weren't really footmen. "Mayhap they're down working upon that fence."

Tilly threw on a bonnet and shawl and ran, but all was quiet in the meadow and neither man was about. Upon her return she popped in at the stables. Papa's horse was still absent. Max was missing as well.

Where could Papa be?

It was true; he had a habit of going off to tend to his flock, but his days as a vicar were over. He had no flock here. He had a housebreaking Riding Officer who'd ransacked their library.

She had good cause to worry.

But where to look? And if she wasn't to go anywhere alone, who might accompany her if Freddy was missing?

She would have to take Edie.

Back in the kitchen, she found the cook bustling about, starting her day's baking. In her short absence, Edie had gone off to the village to fetch more supplies.

It would have to be Wulver accompanying her. They'd first pay a call at Gorse Point Cottage, if she could find her way there.

She had just prepared tea and toast when Pip appeared in the kitchen and wished her a good morning. He headed over to the table where the first pies were cooling.

The cook grunted and swatted his hand and Tilly noticed the paper he clutched.

"Is that a letter, Pip?" She passed him a piece of her toast.

He grinned, accepting her offering and handing her the note. "From the Squire. Almost forgot, miss."

The toast disappeared into his mouth. Tilly gave him a pie and made her escape to the library, eager to read Papa's note in private.

The room was in disarray. With Papa found, she would at least have time to tidy his desk before he returned.

She cracked the seal on the note.

> *My dear girl,*
> *I hope my absence this morning did not alarm you. I was called out last night after you retired and didn't wish to disturb your slumber. It seemed best to wait out the storm's passing and so I received very generous shelter at a neighbor's. I shall return home by-the-by, if not this afternoon, then by the latest, tomorrow when I have every expectation of completing my mission. Have Mr. Smith lodge there until I return, and I'd ask that you not venture out unaccompanied, as we discussed.*
> *You must not worry. All will be as it should.*
> *With love,*
> *Papa*

When Papa had a parish, he was often called away in the night, sometimes for more than one night. But she couldn't imagine Lord Farnsworth calling him away for spiritual sustenance. She must send a note back.

She went to call a servant, remembered that Edie had gone to town, and flew down the stairs to the kitchens.

Pip had left.

Snatching up one of Rose's pies, she returned to the library. It wasn't far to the village. She'd risk walking there unescorted and find someone to carry a note to Gorse Point Cottage.

She cleared a space on Papa's desk and pulled out drawers, looking for writing paper.

At the secret drawer, she paused. She'd left the house plans on her mantel. Perhaps she should retrieve them.

Thoughts of the plans reminded her of the letters. She pulled them from her pocket.

Who are you, Freddy Sanderford?

She scanned the letter from the solicitor again and folded it away. The second letter was from the same solicitor, referencing a payment made for his services.

The third letter, a single sheet covered on one side, bore the elegant hand of a woman, the tight lines of script crossing to save paper. Squinting, she held it up to the light.

> *My dearest Freddy,*
>
> *The funds you sent have been a godsend; I cannot thank you enough for sustaining us through these last months. Your grandmother sends her fond greetings and is hard at work on a warm scarf for you. We have found a lodging in the village, a great boon from a prosperous yeoman to whom your father was always kind. You are not to worry about us, Freddy.*
>
> *I have received a letter from the solicitor you engaged. It may be that he will not be helpful in light of the previous actions taken. I am not at all certain he will be understanding of the assistance I offered your brother, nor that he might not be employed by your brother's enemies. The man in York—oh I fear you are correct and that is*

hopeless. He was the Squire's man through-and-through and put your brother into danger. Tread carefully, oh do. I beg you, I cannot lose another son.

But if it is your destiny to prevail, oh my son, what a glorious day that will be. If I may but have 2 of my 3 sons with me, I shall rejoice. And if you should find the means to restore your fortunes to the state denied your father, grandfather and great-grandfather by that villainous ancestor, your grandmother and I may die happy.

Only do take care. Do not fall into the same trap laid for your brother.

Please write when you may and if you are able to spare some funds—oh, I must not ask. Come to us when you are able. Ask in the village and anyone will direct you.

With love,
Mother

Tilly rested the paper on the desktop.

Good heavens. Freddy's poor mother was living on charity, and in reduced circumstances, while she and her father lived in a manor house with far more bedchambers than they could ever use. They had fuel for their fires, and they still had the wherewithal from Papa's small income and a small bequest from her mother for plain but hardy sustenance.

Plus, they had the hope of an income from Fenwick Manor and its acres and acres of land, and the patronage and financial help of the Earl of Shaldon.

She sat back in Papa's big chair, looking around. They would hire Freddy, perhaps as their steward. And his mother could come as...

A great boon from a prosperous yeoman to whom your father was always kind.

Freddy and his mother were gentry. His mother would not like to be a housekeeper.

Perhaps Fenwick Manor had a cottage where he and his mother could reside.

She glanced at the drawer where the plans should be. She'd been so tired, she'd given short shrift to the grounds and outbuildings last night.

Greggson had been looking for plans of the manor, but what good would those plans have been for him? The hidden library passage hadn't been marked, nor the secret ones she'd traversed with Freddy, nor the muniments room, nor any secret storage areas for smuggling caches.

And for that matter, what good would they do Freddy? He already knew more of the secrets of Fenwick Manor than she did.

And yet Papa had hid the plans away. What else was he hiding?

She idly opened another drawer, feeling around for secret latches and catches. Nothing.

She tried another, and then another.

The third drawer held no secrets either.

She made a circuit of the room, pushing on moldings and latches.

Finally, she returned to the desk and plopped down onto the big chair. Outside, the gray light had shifted, the day having stretched on while she searched. If Papa arrived home soon, this disarray would upset him.

Before tidying, though, she must send that note. He must be informed of the Riding Officer's search of the library, and perhaps then he would come home sooner.

She moved the chair forward and shuffled through papers, looking for a blank sheet that would serve for her note. His latest notebook lay closed, the edge of a paper poking out. A folded parchment had been stuck between blank pages.

She smoothed out the paper.

It was a letter from a solicitor in York, dated some weeks earlier, addressed to their home in Cumberland, and apparently a response to Papa answering questions he'd posed about a gentleman who'd come forward the previous year inquiring about the estate of Sir Richard Fenwick. He'd claimed to be the direct descendant of the true heir of Fenwick manor and was presenting himself on behalf of the elder brother who was in service to the King.

The words niggled at her.

The claimant's great-great-grandfather had been the eldest son of a Baronet Fenwick, believed to have been born out of wedlock. However, the claimant had found a copy of evidence of a marriage making his ancestor's birth legitimate, the original of which he believed had been hidden away by the allegedly bigamous Fenwick line that ended with Sir Richard, and now, Sir Newton.

The claimant's name was Mr. Sanderford, the surname adopted by his ancestor after his rejection by his father.

Tilly fell back in the chair, blood draining from her. The previous night's chill came upon her again in a sudden cold squall.

Freddy Sanderford. Captain Sanderford. The older brother in service to the Crown.

Her heart tumbled about inside her. Freddy had kissed her, warmly too. Warm enough, for a cold-hearted, grasping...She sucked in a breath. He was her cousin, distant, it was true, but a cousin, nonetheless and one who would steal her home out from under her while persuading her to help him bring back his brother.

He was no better than Mr. Greggson, attempting to claim Fenwick Manor, her home, the stout, if shabby, walls that were to provide her secure future. Only, unlike Mr. Greggson, Freddy had made no mention of a marriage that would allow her to remain here.

Perhaps he was after money, some reputed treasure, but what he was truly hunting was the documentation of his ancestor's legitimacy.

Heart pounding, she fingered the ring of keys in her pocket. Surely that last key, the one that fit nowhere else, would work on the locked chest in the alcove. If not, she'd find something to pry open the lid. Freddy had wanted to inspect the contents of all the chests there, and no wonder.

If there was evidence there, she would find it first.

It took a good many minutes of searching and prodding to find the catch for the secret library door, but when she did, she lit a candle and made her way to the small hidden room at the top.

The dust motes floating about the candle and the smell of old cloth and paper made her sneeze. She held her breath inserting the key in the locked chest. The mechanism gave scant resistance. The key turned, the tumbler clicked, and she lifted the lid. Documents lay stacked within, yellowed and cracked, the ribbon and wax fading. She lifted them out, examining each of them less carefully than she would have liked.

They were property documents, deeds and old titles, marriage contracts and dowers, each one telling the story of the grants, and purchases, and marriages that had made Fenwick Manor such a great sprawling estate, each one worthy of closer study—at a later time.

When she reached the bottom of the chest, she sat back on her heels.

There was nothing here about a claimant named Sanderford.

But why would there be? She should have stopped to ask that logical question. Why would Sir Richard and his ancestors have kept documents proving they weren't entitled to Fenwick Manor?

Tilly caught her breath and buried her face in her hands. The baronet who took Fenwick Manor away from Freddy's great-great-whatever wasn't just Sir Richard's ancestor. He was also hers.

She peered into the chest. If the library desk drawer had a false bottom, perhaps this chest did as well.

She poked, and prodded, and pushed at the ornamented corners. One carved rose popped open. She bent closer examining it, then pried at the length of molding it adorned. The molding swung away, and another knob appeared.

She pulled, and a drawer slid out holding a cardboard binder wrapped and tied with a cracked and faded ribbon.

Heart pounding, she eased the ribbon off the package. Several parchments lay inside, the cribbed writing faded in places. She brought the candle closer and squinted.

The first document was a sworn declaration made by a witness to the marriage of George Fenwick, Bt, and Miss Mary Sanderford.

Another declaration followed, and another, all saying the same thing.

Tilly struggled to her feet and braced herself against the open door of the vestment cabinet, heart sinking. The glittering robes worn by the Catholic clergymen who'd served the Fenwicks mocked her.

She wanted a home. She needed a home. A permanent place that would be hers after Papa was gone.

And yet, and yet—she knew right from wrong. Even if Papa had been the rankest of scoundrels and not a gentleman and a man of the cloth, she couldn't perpetuate an old wrong. She couldn't steal what was rightfully another's property.

If Freddy had a claim to this house, the claim must at least be heard. She wouldn't hide these documents. In the time it took the legal process to advance, Papa could finish his book, and then they could live off their income and the sale of his books.

Papa could take in boys and tutor them. Heavens, she knew enough Latin and Greek to teach the youngest ones. They could find a property to let, perhaps even a cottage on Fenwick Manor. Perhaps Freddy—or his mother—would be that generous.

She had scrimped before. She would do it again for the sake of her conscience.

She shoved the file under her arm and made her way back down the secret stairs to the library.

She was arranging books by the secret door when Edie poked her head in.

The girl's gaze swept the room and her nose wrinkled. "'Twas never this much a jumble when Sir Richard was alive."

"Really? It was like this when my father and I arrived. And who do you suppose tossed the books about so?"

"I don't know."

"Or you're not saying. I assume everyone in the village was in here pillaging or knows who was."

The girl's thick brows drew together. "No one knew who the new squire would be. Or if there would be a new squire."

"And Sir Richard being caught spoiled the local free trading industry."

Edie grimaced and pulled a rag from her apron, running it along a shelf. "No. Sir Richard took a good chunk of the profits as his due. Him being captured meant fewer hands in the pie, especially his big paw." She stared at the cloth. "Lord, but there's a year's worth of dust on these shelves."

Tilly went to the desk where she'd placed the packet of documents. "Is my father back?"

"Not yet."

The girl dawdled moving along the stacks.

What neighbor had Papa stayed with? She found a blank page in one of his notebooks and tore it out. She needed to write that note.

Edie sent her a side-wise glance. "Haven't seen the footman either."

Heat flamed in her cheeks. Fortunately, the irritating woman turned away before she could see the blush. Blasted Edie was always discomposing her.

"Did you ever go out with them?" Tilly asked.

"What?"

"When the boats came in. Did you assist with the smuggling?"

Edie's hand stopped moving. "Would I admit it if I did, and me talking to the Justice of the Peace's daughter?"

She'd forgotten her father's new legal authority. And what a joke it was, anyway. Papa would never turn his people in for free trading.

However, as his daughter, she might be able to use his new station to threaten a known housebreaker. If Papa couldn't be bothered with returning home, she could begin an investigation without him.

"Very well. Don't tell me." She paused. "Edie, do you know a village girl named Nelda? She worked here for only a day or two and the ghost drove her away."

She grimaced. "Everyone in the village knows Nelda."

"Yes, I suppose they would. She's Mr. Greggson's..." *Whore? Mistress?* "woman, isn't she? The one you mentioned."

Edie's gaze lifted from the dusting, a careful respect in her eyes.

"I didn't know that when I hired her, else I wouldn't have. Do you know where she lives?"

"She sleeps at the inn most nights, but she has a broken-down hut she calls home on odd days."

Tilly glanced toward the curtained windows. This time of year, the afternoons were short. She'd best write her note. "I'll stop at the inn and talk to her."

"She mayn't be there. I heard Scruggs was looking for her."

"Can you find someone to run a note to Gorse Point Cottage? Your cousin, maybe?"

Edie frowned. "I can take it myself."

CHAPTER EIGHTEEN

"You've left my daughter alone?"

The tone of Sir Newton's rebuke was mild enough, but his face had gone pale.

Freddy had expected he might find Sir Newton ensconced at Gorse Point Cottage, but he'd had to take the chance on coming, anyway. He needed the Earl of Shaldon's aid, and his route to that aid was through Lord Farnsworth.

"The maid and the cook are there. And do you not have a man watching Greggson, Lord Farnsworth?"

Farnsworth blinked.

"Did you not have a man watching him last night?"

Farnsworth blinked again. His long fingers drummed silently on the table. "Why do you ask?"

"Because your daughter found him investigating the library at Fenwick Manor."

"He was *there*?" Sir Newton stood and walked to the fireplace. He let out a long breath. "But she wasn't alone. You were there as well, Freddy?"

"Yes. I...er, happened to be in the kitchens and Tilly called me into battle as it were."

Sir Newton lifted an eyebrow. Blast it, he'd forgotten and used her Christian name.

"So, she is all right?"

"Yes. Greggson jumped out the window. He and his accomplice."

Farnsworth blinked again.

"The inn girl," Freddy said. "Name's Nelda."

Sir Newton's gaze went to Farnsworth. "She didn't tell us that."

Farnsworth sighed. "The lugger wasn't the right bait, and we didn't have the right men watching him. Or her. Brandy?" he asked Freddy.

He shook his head. Clear-thinking was needed, especially around the likes of Farnsworth. "I've found the proof I was looking for. I'd like the Earl's help."

"Proof?" Sir Newton eyed him. "Marriage lines?"

Marriage lines? That old rumor about a secret marriage so long ago had dogged his family for generations. Mother said his brother had found copies of testimonies, though knowing his brother he'd conjured them up himself.

And Sir Newton couldn't possibly have found them. Sir Richard would have destroyed any documents proffered.

Let sleeping dogs and dead ancestors lie, he always believed. The legal wrangling would do naught but fill the coffers of greedy solicitors.

"I know nothing of marriage lines. I found the ledger with Sir Richard's payments to B.G., along with records of casks and cargoes."

"Show me," Lord Farnsworth said.

Freddy took in the dark-eyed man's gaze and the older man's curious one. He'd debated hiding the book some place safe, but he knew he would have to turn it over, eventually. He needed help, and he would have to bring forth the evidence to procure it.

Farnsworth was still a cipher, but he trusted Sir Newton. He drew the ledger from his pocket and handed it over.

Sir Newton let out a breath. "I carried those ledgers to Tilly's bedchamber."

Damn and blast it. His cheeks must be blooming. "Sir," he said, "I would never dishonor your daughter."

Sir Newton leveled a hard look at him.

"I...er...merely escorted her back to her bedchamber and made sure she had a proper fire. After we chased Mr. Greggson and his woman from the manor, she insisted on looking for you in the stables. She was soaked to her bones. I did not molest her."

Sir Newton's lips curved up in a wry smile. "I might rather have hoped you found her irresistible. Poor Tilly."

Poor Tilly? His cheeks must be blazing now. But he'd held so many secrets these past several weeks, he might as well keep one more. He'd never let the passionate moments they'd shared force her hand.

"These notes were here all along," Farnsworth mused.

Farnsworth had seen these ledgers before, or else his people had, and they'd missed this. Someone would pay.

Farnsworth's gaze lifted, his hooded eyes thoughtful. "But we will need further service from you, Captain Sanderford."

The words sent a cold chill through him. Someone would pay, and it would be him.

All his life, there'd been no sure wagers. He'd left for the army knowing his father had two other sons to fall back on to see to his mother's care. Now here he was, the only one left to look after her. He'd done his duty to the Crown, and now that he'd finally come home to clear up his family's muddle, the Crown would come calling again.

He gritted his teeth. "What might that be, my lord?"

"Because of last night's storm, the lugger moved out to sea. It will be here at dusk with a cargo of fine brandy. We just need a ringleader to bribe the Riding Officer." He folded down the lid of a writing desk and pulled out a packet of banknotes.

His heart fell. "I'm not a smuggler," he said.

Farnsworth nodded. "We know that."

"Come lad," Sir Newton said. "You may trust us. You must trust us."

He took in a deep breath. "Perhaps I'd best have that glass of brandy."

When Tilly stepped into the inn's taproom, the chatter went silent.

The lone woman inside was a maid who stopped mid-pour to gawk at her. The rest were men, local laborers and tenants she assumed.

The innkeeper came around the bar and greeted her, unsmiling. His bulk might intimidate a lesser woman.

Fine, it might have intimidated her as well, but she wouldn't give into cowardice. "I'm looking for Nelda."

Scruggs blinked, and pulled her aside, down a short corridor out of earshot of the taproom, if not out of sight.

"The girl hasn't been in," Scruggs said.

She studied the man. No doubt he'd be willing to lie to *her*, the squire's daughter.

"She's not upstairs in one of your bedchambers?" she asked.

He shook his head.

"May I have a look?"

"We've already looked. She's not there."

She lifted an eyebrow. "Not in Mr. Greggson's chambers?"

His ruddy cheeks turned darker. "I run a respectable house."

She scoffed. "And where is the Riding Officer?"

"Gone out some hours since."

"Before or after Nelda left?"

"Here now, miss—"

"Don't you 'here now, miss' me," she hissed. "My father is no Sir Richard, and..."

And what? Papa would turn a blind eye on Nelda's arrangement with Greggson, chalking it up to her ignorance and poverty. He'd go after a corrupt Riding Officer, she knew, but that was none of the innkeeper's affair.

Scruggs bent close. "The girl was here last night and left me with a room full," he whispered in a swirl of gin-breath. "Then Greggson comes in, asks about her, and leaves. Bit later, he storms back in, soaked to the skin and spittin' fire. Wants to know if we seen her. Here all night, he was. Went out late this mornin'. Hasn't come back."

"Did no one investigate her, er, cottage?"

"She weren't there."

But she might be now. Edie had given her directions to Nelda's dwelling. She'd look with her own eyes.

"Thank you." She stepped away, but turned back. "Has Sir Newton been in today?"

He shook his head. "Haven't seen him."

"What about Lord Farnsworth? He's lodging at Gorse Point Cottage."

"Him neither."

Her throat tightened.

"What of a man called Freddy."

"Who?"

"Never mind. He's...not a local man. He's a servant we hired in York."

Scruggs's brow furrowed, and she left him to stew on thoughts of an outsider, someone who might inform, or worse, encroach on his free trading. For now, it was a small revenge against this man who turned a blind eye to Nelda's shame.

She stumbled along in the twilight assessing her choices.

She'd stuffed a candle and tinderbox into one pocket, and a dagger she'd filched from Papa's room into another. The path to Nelda's hovel, as Edie had called it, was no more than a bare line of mud in overgrown brush. If she were a fanciful woman, she'd find herself plagued by some of father's ghosts and goblins.

She wished she had brought the dog.

But Wulver had frightened one too many of the locals, and she didn't wish to risk a commotion in the village. She'd closed Wulver up in the stable with the complaining Max, telling the boy to let the dog out once Tilly was long gone. By that time, Wulver would have lost Tilly's scent. She'd find herself distracted by a hare, or a mole, or some other interesting creature, and forget all about tracking her mistress.

But what if she, Tilly, encountered a creature like Mr. Greggson?

She shook off the worry and plunged ahead. The path took a fork to the left near a thick ancient elm, Edie had said, one she must watch for carefully.

Or not so carefully, as it turned out. The tree loomed over a split in the path like one of the trees of Papa's stories where the fairies swapped out their changeling children.

She bit her lip and picked her way onward. Only a short way now, Edie had said.

Distant voices came to her. A shrill whining overshadowed a man's low tones.

The skin on her neck shivered. The man's voice was not unfamiliar and the deep timbre shook her, sending angry blood rising.

Creeping closer, she reached into her pocket and grasped the hilt of the dagger.

Never would she doubt Edie's descriptive powers. Nelda's dwelling was, truly, a hovel, probably used by some ancient retainer of Fenwick Manor centuries ago.

Gaps in the thatch must let in streams of rain. Broken shutters served in place of glass for the two window openings, and smoke rose from a central hole in the roof.

Keeping to the shadowy brush, she moved close to the window. The shutter hung from one hinge, dim light showing through.

"Tell me, Nelda."

Her breath tightened around her heart, making it hard to take in air. She staggered against a wild sapling. Those tones had been soothing, almost kind. Hadn't she heard their comfort last night.

Freddy—Captain Sanderford—was here. He was working with Nelda.

"Tell me Nelda." Freddy loomed over the diminutive maid, a hair's breadth from the breasts she was trying to smash against his waist. What she lacked in height she made up for in width.

As soon as she opened her mouth, a noise outside caught his attention, and he clamped a hand over Nelda's mouth.

It was no more than a twig snapping.

Greggson. Once he'd left Gorse Point Cottage, he'd been trying all afternoon to track down the man. His last hope had been Nelda.

He tugged the girl along to the nearest corner, away from the window where she promptly fell against him, arms snaking around him like stout vines.

"Dammit," he muttered. She was built like an oversized barrel and strong, probably from having to spar with drunken patrons on a regular basis.

She reached for his shoulder, trying to pull him down to her puckered lips. With another curse, he pushed at her, and was still untangling her tentacles when Tilly burst through the door.

"Get off me." He shoved again, and the shocked girl released him.

He kept a grip on her shoulder and watched Tilly's frown darken.

Hurt glistened in her lovely eyes. "So, this is where you got off to, Cap—"

"Freddy." He cleared his throat and softened his tone, tipping his head to the stout maid who was eyeing the door as if she wanted to bolt. "Just Freddy, miss." Nelda did not need to know his real name. "I've tracked down Greggson's woman here."

"And we're gettin' to know each other." The girl smiled over her shoulder at him and shoved her wide bottom against him.

"Good God." He hefted her by her shoulders and thrust her away. "Miss Fenwick, Nelda here is preparing to tell us what she knows."

"What I know?" Nelda squawked.

"You were in my home last night." Tilly advanced, as fierce and implacable as any proper commander.

That warm place in his heart bloomed again. He hoped she still trusted him.

Nelda lifted her stubby chin. "Says who?"

"I saw you there. What were you looking for?"

"I weren't there."

"Don't you know, Nelda? In Fenwick Manor, there are few rooms that are truly private. There are peepholes and secret passages." She nodded. "Oh yes. Those rumors are true. And I'll give testimony that you broke into my home and were robbing us." Her dark gaze shifted to him. "I'm sure I'll find that something went missing when you and your compatriot visited."

The girl glanced over her shoulder. "It was Freddy. He took it."

Tilly's mouth tightened.

"You numbskull," he said. "I was with Miss Fenwick when we saw you. You and your *accomplice.*"

Nelda had edged toward the door where Tilly stood. She was no match for the little barmaid. Like the ball from a twenty-four pounder, Nelda would blow right over her, out the door and down the path.

He grabbed the girl's arm. "Never mind the housebreaking. Where is Greggson?"

"Greggson?"

"Yes," Tilly said, "and for that matter, where is my father?"

The girl's gaze narrowed on Tilly.

"The squire is missing?"

Tilly bit her lip. "Yes." She nodded. "And while housebreaking and theft is a serious crime, capital murder—of a baronet and Justice of the Peace, most assuredly will be a hanging offense."

Bravo. Tilly was improvising. Even in this dim light, he could see Nelda's face visibly pale, her cocky swagger evaporating. "He was aright this morn when they cut me loose," she whispered.

Tilly grabbed the girl's other arm. "He caught up with you after you ransacked the manor?"

Nelda's gaze searched their faces, and she made a pathetic whimpering noise. "I was walking last night in the rain and twisted my ankle. Out of nowhere, here's the squire, lending me a hand. Only, it wasn't really a hand, and there was more with him. His lordship as is staying over at Gorse Point, and some others."

He took Tilly's arm, completing the circle. "He's with Farnsworth," he said. "He's safe."

Tilly nodded. "I won't lie in my testimony. I saw you and Mr. Greggson searching the library after breaking into our home. You will certainly be transported."

"Or hang," he said. "I think you will hang. Breaking into the house of a Justice of the Peace to search for evidence against your criminal partner."

"*I won't hang,*" Nelda cried. "John Black was only transported. Housebreaking ain't so bad as what he did."

"John Black's mother bribed the judge to save her son's life," he said.

Next to him, Tilly stiffened.

Oh hell. His mother had sold her security and her future to mitigate the sentence and spare his brother a hanging. He hadn't meant to give that away.

"I don't imagine *your* mother will bribe a judge," he said. It was cruel, and he didn't care. Nelda had been complicit in his brother's downfall.

The girl's mouth dropped, and she peered closer. "You," she whispered. "He's been looking for you. Freddy...Frederick. You're the brother."

"John Black's brother," Tilly said. "Or rather, brother to the man who carried the real John Black's crimes all the way to the antipodes."

Nelda bit her lip. "It weren't right what he did."

"No. It wasn't," Tilly said. "Sir Richard was evil."

The girl shook her head. "Not him. That is, not just him."

She meant Greggson. Damn it, he needed to move this along. He needed the girl to get a message to Greggson.

Outside, the brush shook in a rush of clopping hooves.

"He's here." Nelda began to tremble. "Don't let him hurt me."

"Stop whimpering. Go out and tell him to meet me."

"Where?"

"The glen. You know the one. Where the hound appears."

Nelda's eyes widened. "Where the treasure is?"

Tilly shot him a look.

The glen, with its fissures, its route to the sea, and its fearsome hound—he'd heard the wild claim of hidden gold even before reading Sir Newton's notes. The only treasures stowed in the crevice were meager casks of brandy and gin, and none of them recent. Some lone free trader had stashed them and then passed on and forgotten them. The glen held no treasure, but it was a wonderful place on a moonless night for a smuggler to pay a bribe.

He pushed Tilly to the corner, yanked the door open and shoved Nelda outside.

CHAPTER NINETEEN

Tilly staggered against the wall while a commotion raged.

She looked up to see Freddy gripping the girl, a pistol barrel planted in her back.

"You can't just do what you're told, can you Nelda?" Freddy said.

"Ah, the footman," Greggson said. "Hiding behind a woman? James, wasn't it?"

"It's him," Nelda squawked. "The one you're looking for."

A pistol exploded and Freddy fell back pulling the girl and the door with him. The crude bar dropped into place.

Nelda collapsed in front of the door.

"You shot her?"

"Shhh." Freddy stepped over the girl and moved next to her. "Feel this." He held up the pistol and she wrapped her hand around it. It was cold. "The shot hit the door frame. She's fainted, or faking, unless a piece of lead ricocheted into that thick skull of hers."

Nelda stirred, giving credence to his words.

"Why were you here?" Tilly asked.

"Shhh. I don't want him to find you. They're laying a trap."

"They?" Tilly's head was spinning.

The door rattled, and he shushed her.

They. Papa and Lord Farnsworth.

Good heavens.

"Open up, Nelda," Greggson said. "There's a good girl."

"She's dead," Freddy said. "You've killed her."

The sound came from farther away. Freddy was already moving toward the flapping window shutter.

Nelda moaned and struggled up on her elbows.

Blood dribbled from the girl's forehead. Tilly snatched the girl's cap and mopped at it.

"*Aargh.*"

The bellow had come from the window. Freddy twisted the arm poking through, and a pistol flew and exploded. Wood splintered and cracked, and Greggson swore, tumbling through the window onto Freddy. Both men struggled and scrambled up, facing off. Greggson's right hand dangled oddly, but his left clutched a saber.

"You," he said to Tilly. "What are you doing here?"

"I'll ask you the same. *I'm* investigating a housebreaking at Fenwick Manor. And..." Her father wasn't truly missing, but perhaps Greggson didn't know that. And Freddy was sliding into the shadows where the broken shutter lay while they talked. "My father has not returned home. Where is my father? Perhaps both *crimes* are related."

Greggson's gaze narrowed. "How should I know where your father is? You shouldn't be here, and not with that man. Why, do you know—"

Crack. The broken shutter landed squarely on Greggson's head and he went down.

Tilly glanced at Freddy. Did she know what? Who Freddy was?

Of course, she did. He was the man who would take her home from her.

"He's only stunned." Freddy lifted the bar from the door and hauled Nelda to her feet. "If Sir Newton and Farnsworth freed you this morning, I'll risk doing the same. Go back to the inn and stay there. Scruggs will look after you, and you must give testimony against the Riding Officer."

He took Tilly's hand. "Come on."

"Wait. Where are we going?"

"He's only stunned. He'll be up and after us in a moment." He untied Greggson's horse.

"Sanderford," Greggson called. "Don't trust him, Matilda."

Matilda. No one called her Matilda, no one who truly knew her. She gulped in great breaths and tried to quell her shaking.

Greggson must think her a weak pea-goose, assaulting her as a way to force marriage and take Fenwick Manor. For certain, Greggson was a villain.

Freddy was after her home as well, though he hadn't offered to take her as his wife. In fact, she'd come upon in him Nelda's arms, that was certain as well.

She took a step back from him. "Where are we going?"

"*We* are not..." Freddy glanced back at the hut. "Oh hell, he might go after you first if I send you off." He slapped the horse's rump, sending it running. "The glen."

He said that loudly enough that Greggson surely heard.

Freddy wanted Greggson to go there. Had Papa truly laid a trap for the Riding Officer? Perhaps he'd be waiting in the glen with Lord Farnsworth, two older gentlemen against the younger man. Greggson was injured, but he still had his cutlass.

She turned down the path and ran. Footsteps pounded behind her.

When she reached the elm, a great beast jumped out at her, knocking her back into Freddy's arms.

Wulver. Two paws rested on each of her shoulders, and a wet tongue lapped her cheek.

"Down," Freddy ordered and Wulver obeyed.

She obeyed immediately and without question. Because she liked Freddy, and trusted him. That was another fact that was certain.

Freddy's arms tightened around her and his breath tickled her ear. "We must get to the glen before him," he whispered.

Wulver's head lifted and she growled at the path they had come down.

"Come, love." Freddy pulled her off the path.

Gripping her hand, he rushed sure-footed down a path only he could see, swerving around bushes and stones, and fallen branches.

How could he be so sure of his way? She couldn't catch her breath to ask.

Finally, they broke through to another path, one she recognized as the road she and Papa had taken the night they'd visited here.

If Greggson took the roundabout way, they would beat him by several minutes.

Freddy's pace never slowed until they reached the dip in the road that signaled the route to the glen. Once there, she shook off his hand and sucked in deep breaths.

His arm came around her and he led her into the dark vale.

The smell of the sea and the distant crash of waves reached them, along with a chilling wind that seemed to whistle up through the earth. And it was dusk, the gloaming, with darkness seeping through bare branches and deepening the shadows.

Freddy stopped near a fallen log.

"What is this trap?" she whispered. "You, and Nelda—"

"No. I...no. Not me and Nelda. And Greggson is the villain here."

"Oh really, Captain Frederick Sanderford, claimant to the Fenwick baronetcy?"

"*No.* No, Tilly. You know about that? That was my brother's folly, and look what it got him. I want him back. I want my family restored."

"By claiming your rightful inheritance."

"*No.*" He pulled her deeper into the shadows and put his mouth to her ear. "By getting justice for him. That story about us and the Fenwicks...my mother fed it to us with our daily porridge. It's ridiculous. A fairy tale. Nothing can be proven, and even if it—"

"What if I have the proof?"

"It means nothing." He tugged her and when she stumbled, wrapped her up in his arms so tightly she could feel the beat of his pulse.

"Let me go."

He gazed down at her, his lips almost touching hers. "Fenwick Manor is yours. Fighting over it would cost money I need to save my brother."

She fought for a breath. "And if I have the proof?"

He paused, so close she could taste his breath. Somewhere in his search for her father he'd stopped for a brandy. And there was still enough light to make out a glint in his eyes.

He let out a breath and leaned closer. "Burn it. Or put it back where you found it. I'll keep the secret."

He touched his lips to hers, gently and then more firmly, melting her more than either kiss had the night before. His hand swept down her back and she angled her lips for a deeper kiss, and...

Heart pounding, she eased away a fraction. "But, but, one day, your son—"

"No."

His lips found her neck, and she bent her head, sighing. "Papa has not renounced Holy Orders. You can give him the living, or allow us a cottage on the estate." The sheep were coming. She could manage them for the true squire.

"Take your home? Oh, Tilly. Someday...some worthy man will win you and what about your children, Tilly?"

"This Fenwick line will end with me."

Freddy's mouth firmed. "Never say that." Calloused fingers stroked her cheek. "If...I would..." He sucked in a breath and pressed her head to his shoulder, their hearts pounding together. She held her breath. *If you would what?*

"There is another solution." The quiet voice came from behind them and they both turned. Papa rose in the shadows and brushed the back of his trousers. He'd been sitting on the fallen log, hidden by the encroaching darkness.

Tilly flew at him and gripped his hands. "You scared me half witless," she said. "Never do that again."

He chuckled softly and nodded at Freddy. "Captain Sanderford, there is a way to get Fenwick Manor back into the hands of the rightful family in one generation with no legal fuss or bother in that regard."

Papa was giving up. Of course he was. He would turn Fenwick Manor over to the Sanderfords. He would do the right thing.

Tears welled, and she beat them back. Justice required this be accomplished.

The brush crackled like a wild animal was thrashing through, and Tilly was yanked back into the shadows, a hand covering her mouth.

Greggson crashed through the thicket, his saber raised.

Freddy saw the flash of steel before he could take in the man. He raised both hands and backed up. Without knowing where Tilly stood, he wouldn't draw his pistol.

She and her father had disappeared, and thank God for it. Moments before, he'd almost said the words: *marry me*. Until his brother was safe, until he had something to offer, he wouldn't ask for her promise.

But he'd die before he'd see this maggot lay a hand on her or Sir Newton.

Wulver prowled out of the bushes, dark and snarling.

"Wulver." Freddy eased out his pistol and beckoned the dog. "Steady girl. Greggson, I have your money."

"What money?"

"The usual. Same as you took from Sir Richard."

"What have you done with Miss Fenwick?"

"Miss Fenwick has run along home to Sir Newton."

"And why is the beast here?"

"Don't you know? Look at her. Wulver feels drawn to the lair of the hell-hound."

"And the lair of the demon smuggler?"

Freddy scoffed. "As you say. Now, there's a boat arriving tonight." He reached a free hand into his coat and pulled out a wad of banknotes. "You'll go back to your snug bed at the inn and let my men offload, there's a good chap."

"Or perhaps I'll just kill you and take your money and my bounty on the cargo."

Freddy shrugged. "Was not your partnership with Sir Richard profitable? Ours could be the same."

Greggson chuckled deep in his throat. "Why be a lackey again when I can have Fenwick Manor and Sir Richard's entire enterprise in my grasp?"

Rage boiled in him. He knew what the man meant—he thought to force a marriage with Tilly and do away with her father if he interfered with his plans.

"You mean that instead of simply taking bribes, you plan to run all of the smuggling from Scarborough to Whitby?"

"What if I do?"

"I've a boat coming in. Take the money or don't." He tossed the packet on the ground.

Greggson bent and grimaced as he snatched it up with his bad hand. "You'll double this."

"Will I? What will I get in return?"

"For now? I won't kill you."

Greggson wouldn't kill him because both of his pistols were gone and his right hand was limp. Not broken, probably, but badly sprained.

Wulver's menacing growl rumbled from deep in her belly and all of her fur stood on end. The saber came up, and he grabbed the dog's collar.

*****

"Shhh," Papa whispered into her ear, finally moving his hand from her mouth.

There was no need to strain to hear the conversation. It was only a wonder that Wulver hadn't given away their presence. She could almost feel the ground trembling with the dog's growls.

"How do you plan to run all the smuggling from Scarborough to Whitby if you run about shooting the local free traders?"

Why be a lackey again when I can have Fenwick Manor and Sir Richard's entire enterprise in my grasp.

If Freddy was working with both Papa and Farnsworth to get the truth out of Greggson, then Lord Farnsworth was somewhere hereabouts.

"How do you think Sir Richard maintained his control?"

"By murder? The Justice of the Peace?"

Greggson's harsh laugh sent a shiver down her spine.

"Aye, well, the current Justice of the Peace won't pay any mind to a smuggler being killed, unless there's a ghost, or a goblin involved."

"I think you are wrong, Greggson. I think you have underestimated the new Squire. Sir Newton will never allow the killing."

"If you haven't noticed, Sir Newton is not long for this world."

"His daughter will never allow it."

Greggson laughed. "She'll do what I say once we're married."

Oh, that was too much. Tilly broke from her father's grasp and plunged into the clearing.

"How *dare* you, Greggson," she said.

*****

No Tilly.

Before Freddy could shout a warning, Greggson had turned his blade at her. The powerful dog wrenched out of his hand and pounced.

Like a soldier with battle lust, like a hound of hell, Wulver roared. Greggson stumbled back, but his blade came down, and the dog squealed.

Tilly dove at the dog. Scrambling up, Greggson thrust again, but Freddy parried the blade with his pistol and slammed the butt into Greggson's head, shoving him to the ground and pinning his saber arm.

He punched him, again and again and again while a rebounding Wulver snapped at the man's writhing legs.

"Enough." A boot came down on Greggson's arm, someone wrenched the saber away, and Freddy was pulled to his feet.

Heart racing, he struggled for breath.

Farnsworth appeared and two of his men came forward, hauling up Greggson. Wulver's jaws were still clamped to the Riding Officer's leg.

"Get it off," Greggson said. "I'll kill it, I swear."

Tilly grabbed Wulver's collar. "Lay a hand on my dog and you'll pay a steep price."

Freddy's fists clenched. He'd fought to the death before, and he would have killed Greggson now if Farnsworth had not pulled him off of him. "Kill the dog, and I'll kill you."

"No lady of mine would keep such a hound."

Tilly scoffed. "No lady would keep *you*."

Freddy's hand covered Tilly's on Wulver's collar. She glanced at him, her gaze softening.

"Is our hell-hound all right?" Sir Newton asked.

"Sir Newton?" Greggson's eyes narrowed. "Lord Farnsworth?"

In the way of corrupt men everywhere, Greggson was not a total fool. He was realizing his trap and contemplating a way to wriggle out of it.

"Mr. Greggson has taken his bribe," Freddy said. "For the boat coming in."

"Not true. Will you assist me, Sir Newton, in arresting this man?"

"Arrest me? And then what? Have me transported and keep the goods for yourself?" Freddy ran a hand over the dog's wiggling flank. Her wound appeared to be minor. "And there's the treasure I found here in the glen. I suppose you'll take that for yourself?"

Farnsworth watched the proceedings.

Sir Newton set a hand upon Tilly's shoulder. "Is it the Viking gold or the Roman you've found, Captain?"

Greggson started and glared. "There's no treasure. Just a story to lure your daughter to the glen. I saw him pull her into the brush."

"Oh, there's treasure, all right," Sir Newton beamed a smile from Freddy to Tilly. "I know you recognize the name Sanderford, Mr. Greggson.

As you know, Captain Sanderford has claims on Fenwick Manor."

"A very credible claim." Tilly's voice cracked.

"Claims, my dear," Sir Newton said, nodding to Freddy. "Plural."

The scent of lilac and lemon drifted to him, and longing filled him. He wouldn't claim Fenwick Manor. He'd never cast the brave lass out of her home. "I've told you—"

"There's more, Greggson." Lord Farnsworth said quietly. "He also has a brother wrongly prosecuted and transported in place of Sir Richard."

"I've said I know nothing about that," Greggson said.

"Fortunately," Sir Newton said, "we won't have to rely on your word. We have evidence. Will you have your men lock him up, Farnsworth? I believe I'll take up my duties as Justice of the Peace now."

As Farnsworth and his men dragged a protesting Greggson away, Sir Newton's smile took in both him and Tilly.

"As I was saying, Freddy, there is a way to get Fenwick Manor back into the hands of the rightful family in one generation with little legal fuss or bother."

Tilly bent down and stroked the dog. "I found the marriage documents. The ones proving your entitlement."

He heard tears in her voice, but when she looked at him she was dry-eyed and tense.

"Your mother and grandmother must come to Fenwick Manor."

Blast it. The letters. He'd completely forgotten about them. Clearly she hadn't.

He raked a hand through his hair. "My mother?"

She nodded. "And grandmother. And if Papa and I may have a cottage—"

"A cottage?"

"Yes."

"You think I could throw you and the Squire out of your home—"

"It is properly your home." She gulped, and he saw the tears then, glistening in the half-light.

He couldn't abide tears, and neither, he suspected, could she. "Don't be a nodcock."

"A *nodcock*?"

"Yes. Don't you dare start weeping. You are the mistress of Fenwick Manor and will always be so."

Sir Newton chuckled. "*Gie me the hour o' gloamin' grey, It maks my heart sae cheery O, To meet thee on the lea-rig, My ain kind Dearie O.*"

Tilly rolled her eyes. "Burns," she whispered.

When he looked, Sir Newton was heading down the path, one hand firmly leading the dog away. At the bend in the path, the older man looked back, and though night was falling, he could swear the squire winked.

There is a way to get Fenwick Manor back into the hands of the rightful family in one generation with little legal fuss or bother in that regard.

A tiny buzzing started in his head and he grasped Tilly's shoulders. Gad, he was willing. He'd held back from temptation the night before, only because he was a gentleman and she was a more than worthy lady, and…and he cared for her. He loved her.

His hands firmed and he inwardly shook himself. She must know everything first.

"Your father was setting up Greggson," he said. "They knew he was corrupt, and they asked me to assist." The buzzing moved to his ears. "They knew who I was. At least, they knew I was the brother of the man transported. I didn't know they knew about my family's claim."

"Of course, they did." Her gaze searched his, her eyes deep and luminous. "At least, Papa knew. He was corresponding with a solicitor."

"My brother approached Sir Richard's solicitor, who notified Sir Richard. The old squire was in peril from an honest Revenue Officer down the coast looking to stop the string of murders committed by John Black's gang. Sir Richard snatched up my brother and solved his two legal problems in one sweep."

"Your mother truly did bribe the judge?"

"Or else he would have been hanged."

She touched a hand to his cheek. "Oh Freddy. Did Papa know you were living in our attic? I wonder." She bit her lip. "Freddy, we are cousins."

He took in a breath that brought another taste of lilac and lemon. "Third or fourth cousins at best. Perhaps even once or twice removed. Practically unrelated."

Her lips trembled. Whether she would smile or shed tears, he couldn't be sure.

"Tilly," he said, "Your father knows I was in your bedchamber last night and he didn't berate me."

"Oh." She shook her head. "Papa is full of surprises. He's left us alone in the gloaming."

"There's that as well." He dropped to his knee. "Miss Fenwick, there's only one solution to this dilemma. Please marry me."

"Did Papa suggest this to you earlier? This 'way to get Fenwick Manor back into the hands of the rightful family in one generation with little legal fuss'?"

The sadness in her voice tore at his heart. He stood and pulled her into his arms. "Fenwick Manor is in the hands of the rightful family, the family that appreciates all its history, and, er, *quirks*, and I would like the mistress of Fenwick Manor to be in the hands of the rightful man, the man who appreciates her, the man who adores her."

He kissed her, as tenderly as he was able given the need to sweep her away and ravish her, and then pressed his forehead to hers. "Your answer, Miss Tilly?"

She let out a long breath. "And can the man tolerate *her* quirks?"

"The man adores them."

"Oh, Freddy. Yes."

She lifted her chin and fell into him, and they kissed while the light faded to full dark, and the distant sea roared, and the fog settled around them. They kissed until a wet nose pressed against him and two wet paws landed, one on her shoulder and one on his.

Freddy laughed and removed his hand from inside her gown and straightened her bodice. "Chaperoned by a hell-hound. We shall have to find her a suitable mate."

"Poor Max. He'll quit if we have more dogs like her."

Freddy laughed again. "They'll be puppies first. Max will fall in love with them. Fenwick Manor must have its hell-hounds."

She raised an eyebrow. "So...a pack of hell-hounds will ensure Sir Richard's ghost has been thoroughly vanquished and will no longer haunt the staff?"

He heard the smile in her voice and pulled her close. "I assure you," he said, "His ghost has been thoroughly vanquished." And he kissed her again.

But he intended to haunt Miss Tilly Fenwick for as long as they both should live.

Winter had faded into early spring with the promise of flowers blooming and new lambs.

And another generation of Fenwicks.

Tilly rubbed her swelling belly and then fondled Wulver's ear. There would also be puppies soon. What they would look like was anyone's guess.

She made her way down to the meadow where Freddy and Papa stood leaning against their stone fence chatting, no doubt about some story they'd heard in the village taproom the night before. As in his days as a vicar, Papa was spending a great deal of time with the local people, hearing their stories and troubles, and bringing their concerns to the new master of Fenwick Manor.

Freddy had taken her hand and her name, and would soon be awarded the house and land and holdings of Fenwick Manor—soon being a relative term in legal processes. He would not be Sir Frederick until Papa died.

They were all happy with that arrangement, even Freddy's mother and grandmother who'd approved of the resolution of that ancient injustice, and taken up residence under the same roof.

They were still waiting for word on the other injustice.

Freddy spotted her and came to kiss her cheeks. "Three more lambs born today. You shall have to decide on a larger grazing ground soon." He rapped the dog on her head. "And you, Wulver are on duty against foxes."

Papa rubbed his stomach. "I'll be off to see what Rose has baked today. I shall catch up with you in girth soon, Tilly." With a hearty laugh, he walked up the hill to the house.

A *clip-clop* of a rider brought their attention to the lane and Tilly groaned. The new Riding Officer was a sober, dedicated fellow who visited the manor far too often for a glimpse of Edie. The man would never take a bribe and was rather clueless about Papa and Freddy's policy of winking at a barrel of gin here or there. And heaven help him if he thought to convert Edie to his Methodist ways.

"It's an express rider." Freddy dropped her hand and ran to meet the fellow who quickly handed him a packet.

She waddled down the road to join him, meeting him halfway.

"News?"

His tense expression told her it might be good news or bad.

"Open it," she said.

A drop of rain plopped onto her bonnet, and Freddy shoved the packet into his coat.

"Come." He pulled her along the short distance to his formerly secret entrance, hurriedly opening the door, and lighting the lamp he kept nearby.

"Your mother will—"

"Let's make sure it's good news first."

She let him tug her along up the stairs, but instead of stopping at the kitchen, he went on, pausing only to let her catch her breath. They came out in the attics and went into his old hidden chamber.

He handed her the letters. One was from Lord Farnsworth, the other from the solicitor the Earl of Shaldon had engaged for the task at hand.

They owed much to the Earl's beneficence.

"Open them, Freddy."

He sighed and snapped the seal on Farnsworth's letter, scanning the lines, a smile blooming on his face and he whooped, spinning her around.

"He's coming home?"

"Yes. They found him in reasonably good health. He's on a ship as we speak, on his way home."

Her arms went around him. Freddy would have his brother back and sooner than they expected.

Sooner than was possible. She stepped back. "But the journey is many months. How—"

"They set the process in motion months ago, after Sir Richard's death and as soon as they learned the judge had been bribed."

The judge had been bribed twice, once by Sir Richard, who had the man in his pocket, and then by Freddy's mother to spare her son from the gallows.

"Is your mother in legal peril?"

"No. Farnsworth has even seen to that."

Thank heavens. Bribing a judge was no small offense.

"And what is in the solicitor's letter?"

He scanned the paper. "More detail of what Farnsworth has said."

"Come, let's go tell your mother."

Freddy moved in front of the door. "This is grandmama's nap time. We should wait for her." He lifted her hand and kissed the palm. "You've always found that bed in the corner comfortable."

Her cheeks flamed, still, even after so many months of marriage. She and Freddy had enjoyed the comforts of that cot frequently when they were meant to be cataloguing the contents of the muniments room next door.

The cataloguing was nowhere near complete, but they had the rest of their lives to work on it. Or perhaps they would leave it, and the next generation of Fenwicks could see to it.

She stepped into his embrace. "Greggson foiled. Your brother rescued. The true Fenwick line restored. What will you accomplish next, husband? Finding a hidden treasure?"

"No need." He tugged her shawl away and nuzzled her neck. "The treasure was hidden right under our noses, and I've found it."

"*What?*"

A wicked gleam glowed in his eyes, one that warmed her inside and made her heart melt. One she'd grown used to these last several months.

His gaze went to her lips. "More precious than rubies, my dear." And he swept her up into a kiss that promised many more.

The End

If you enjoyed this story, please consider leaving a review at Goodreads, BookBub, or Amazon.

A Note from the Author

Did you notice the Common Elements Romance Project logo on the cover and wonder what that is? Over one hundred romance authors have come together to write stories that have just five things in common:

- A lightning storm
- Lost keys
- A haunted house (really haunted or rumored to be)
- A stack of thick books
- A person named Max

Our stories are not connected and can be read in any order. Plus, they run the gamut of romance sub-genres and heat levels, so there's something for everyone.

If you've read *The Counterfeit Lady*, you'll recognize Fenwick Manor. In *Haunting Miss Fenwick,* not only is there a happily ever after for our hero and heroine, but for the ancient manor itself. This story was so much fun to write!

Thanks go to author Cora Lee, the force behind the Common Elements Project, to my editor Tessa Shapcott, and to my supportive family, especially my husband.

I love hearing from readers! You can contact and follow me on Facebook, Twitter, Pinterest, and Goodreads. And my latest news is always available at my website, https://AlinaKField.com.

For special notices about sales and other news, please consider signing up for my newsletter at my website. I promise I won't spam you or sell your email address!

Best regards and happy reading!

Alina K. Field

Also by Alina K. Field

Sons of the Spy Lord Series
Available in print and eBook

The Bastard's Iberian Bride
Book One
2017, Havenlock Press

For a chance at true freedom, a spy's daughter dodges an
arranged marriage to an earl's illegitimate son and seeks the
fortune left by her inscrutable father.

The Viscount's Seduction
Book Two
2017, Havenlock Press

Lady Sirena Hollister has lost everything, even her fey
abilities. But when the fairies hand her a chance at a
London Season, her schemes for revenge stir up an
unknown enemy, and spark danger of a different sort,
in the person of a handsome Viscount.

The Rogue's Last Scandal
Book Three
2017, Havenlock Press

Falling—literally—into the arms of the *ton*'s most
outrageous rogue seems a risky path of escape, but
Maria Graciela Kingsley y Romero has no other
choice. Only England's greatest spy lord can help her,
and he is not to be found—so his son will have to do!

The Counterfeit Lady
Book Four
2018, Havenlock Press

Vowing she'll never submit to an arranged marriage, an earl's daughter bolts for the seaside cottage that will someday be hers. But she finds her quiet refuge occupied by the last man she ever wants to see—an American artist, who's a thief, and quite possibly one of her father's spies.

Avenging the Earl's Lady
Book Five
2018, Havenlock Press

The long war is over, but honor requires vanquishing one last enemy, and the Earl of Shaldon has no time for romance. But when the lady he longs for interferes in his plot, and his enemy strikes at her, nothing else matters but avenging his lady.

Novellas and Holiday Stories

The Marquess and the Midwife
A Christmas Novella
Finalist, 2016 National Reader's Choice Award
2016, Havenlock Press

Uncovering a lie drives a new marquess back from a self-imposed exile at Christmas to find the only woman he's ever loved. Finding her turns out to be easy, uncovering her stunning secrets, a bit harder. But winning her back will be the greatest challenge of all.

Available in print and eBook

A Leap Into Love
A Sweet Regence Romance Novella
2018, Havenlock Press

Can a gentleman be too charming? The ladies of
Upper Upton think so.

When the single ladies of the village conspire to teach
their charmer a lesson that might bankrupt him, the
town's loveliest young widow—who's sworn off
marriage forever—steps up to warn him.

A Leap Into Love is a short sequel to *The Marquess
and the Midwife*

Available on Kindle

Liliana's Letter
Finalist, 2015 National Reader's Choice
Award
2015, Havenlock Press

The Matchmaker Meets the Matchbreaker

Liliana Ashford's future as a professional chaperone
depends on her wealthy charge's successful marriage,
but her own close encounter with a scoundrel years
ago makes her determined to save the girl from the
same kind of rogue.

Available in print and eBook

The Ghost of Depford Hall
A short, sweet Halloween sequel to
Liliana's Letter
2017, Havenlock Press

It's her mother's last All Hallows' Eve.

When family, friends, and tenants gather,
goblins, ghouls, and ghosts are banned from this
All Hallows' Eve party.

Only, no one told the Ghost of Depford Hall!

Available on Kindle

Bella's Band
A 2015 RONE Award Finalist
2014, Soul Mate Publishing

*A spinster's secrets tempt a killer—and steal
a soldier's heart.*

Saddled with his brother's title and debts,
nothing about this new life makes the Earl of
Hackwell want to stay—until he meets a lady
with a secret that can change everything.

Available on Kindle

Rosalyn's Ring
2014 Book Buyer's Best Winner, Novella Category
2013, Soul Mate Publishing

When a young woman is put up for auction in a wife sale, Rosalyn Montagu seizes the chance to rescue her—and to recover a treasured family heirloom, her father's signet ring. Her plans are thwarted by the newly anointed Viscount Cathmore who finds her provoking beauty, upper crust manner, and larcenous streak intriguing. Her secrets rouse his jaded heart, including the truth of her identity—she is the woman whose home he has usurped. But more mysteries swirl around Rosalyn's past, and Cathmore is just the man to help her uncover the truth.

Available on Kindle

www.ingramcontent.com/pod-product-compliance
Lightning Source LLC
Chambersburg PA
CBHW061152170626
46809CB00003B/1061